FARMING ENCYCLOPEDIAS

THE FARM ANIMAL ENCYCLOPEDIA

BY SAMANTHA S. BELL

Encyclopedias

An Imprint of Abdo Reference

abdobooks.com

TABLE OF CONTENTS

KEEPING FARM ANIMALS 4
ALPACAS 6
BEES 14
BISON 22
CAMELS 30
CATS 38
CATTLE 46
CHICKENS 54
DOGS 62
DONKEYS 70
DUCKS 78
FISH 86
GEESE 94
GOATS 102
HORSES 110
LLAMAS 118

OSTRICHES.. 126
PIGS.. 134
QUAIL... 142
RABBITS... 148
REINDEER... 156
SHEEP.. 164
TURKEYS..172
WATER BUFFALO................................ 180
GLOSSARY 188
TO LEARN MORE................................ 189
INDEX 190
PHOTO CREDITS.................................191

KEEPING FARM ANIMALS

There are many kinds of farms. Most are family-owned farms. These are categorized as small, medium, or large farms, depending on how much they earn. Others are large commercial farms.

Both family-owned and commercial farms raise animals. These include familiar livestock such as cattle, pigs, and sheep. But they can also include exotic livestock, such as alpacas, bison, and camels. Even bees are often considered livestock. Some farms raise fowl such as chickens, ducks, and turkeys. The types of animals on a farm may be determined by the climate, the size of the farm, and available food sources.

Farmers must take care of their animals' needs, which include food, water, shelter, and medical care.

Eggs and bacon are two food products that come from farm animals.

When choosing animals, farmers also consider the products the animals produce. These products help the farmer earn income. The farm can provide jobs for other people too. In this way, the livestock industry plays an important role in the global economy. Altogether, it supports the livelihoods of more than one billion people.

Livestock, farm animals kept for profit, provide nourishment for people around the world. This is especially true in developing countries. In some of these countries, many people do not have enough food to eat every day. For them, raising their own livestock helps them survive during difficult times. Meat and other animal products supply essential nutrients such as iron, zinc, vitamin A, and vitamin B12. A 2019 report found that livestock supply 34 percent of the protein consumed worldwide.

Farm animals serve people in other ways too. They provide power when machines are not available or practical. They help get rid of rodents and other pests. They protect livestock or property. Their manure can become fertilizer for crops. Products such as fiber and leather come from livestock. Farm animals are an essential part of people's everyday lives.

ALPACAS

Alpacas are members of the Camelidae family, which also includes llamas and camels. Although alpacas and llamas look similar, llamas are much larger animals. Alpacas weigh between 120 and 200 pounds (55 to 90 kg). They are about half the size of llamas.

Alpacas come from the Andes mountain regions of Chile, Peru, and Bolivia in South America. Thousands of years ago, Andean people captured and bred wild animals called vicuñas. Historians believe the people bred vicuñas for the traits they liked best. The animals they bred were calmer around people. They grew more hair, which people could use. This domesticated animal became the alpaca. Wild vicuñas still roam the high-altitude plains in South America.

Alpaca fur is also called fleece or wool. The Andean people have long prized alpaca fleece. The Inca people

There are more than 260,000 alpacas in the United States registered with the Alpaca Owners Association.

Peru has more vicuñas than any other South American country.

of the Andes allowed only royalty to wear robes made of alpaca fleece.

Alpacas have been in the United States since the 1980s. Since then, most of the country's alpaca farmers have established their farms in the western United States. The states with the most alpacas include Colorado, California, Oregon, and Washington.

The suri's fleece grows longer than the fleece of the huacaya, *second from right*. Suri fleece can get long enough to touch the ground.

PURPOSE

Today alpacas are still raised for their fleece. There are two breeds of alpacas. The most common are called huacayas. They make up 85 to 90 percent of all alpacas. Huacayas have dense, soft, wavy fleece on most of their body. Suri alpacas are rarer. They have long, silky fur that hangs down along their sides.

A single alpaca produces 5 to 10 pounds (2.3 to 4.5 kg) of fleece each year. The fleece has qualities that benefit both the alpacas and people who use it. Each hair is hollow and full of air. These air pockets absorb water. The fleece wicks away sweat in hot weather. In wet weather, it keeps moisture

away from the skin. In cold weather, body heat warms the air pockets. This makes the fleece a great insulator.

Some people prefer alpaca fleece to sheep's wool. Sheep's wool contains an oil called lanolin. It can be irritating to the skin. But alpaca fleece does not contain lanolin, so it causes less irritation. It feels softer and warmer than sheep's wool.

Alpaca fur is popular for being both lightweight and warm.

Alpaca fleece has a variety of natural colors, including white, beige, brown, black, and gray. Light-colored fleece can be easily dyed to make more colors. Yarn from the fleece is used to make sweaters, blankets, hats, and scarves.

In some places, alpacas are also raised for their meat. The meat is higher in protein and lower in fat and cholesterol than beef, chicken, or salmon. In Peru, people eat alpaca meat the same way Americans eat beef. It can be served as a steak, and it can be grilled or breaded.

One reason alpaca fleece feels softer than sheep's wool is because alpaca fleece is thinner and smoother.

Customers can buy alpaca meat directly from some alpaca farms.

In the United States, alpaca meat is starting to become more popular. But farmers earn more money from the fleece. Farmers will remove alpacas that do not have the right quality or color of wool from their herd. The farmer may decide to slaughter these alpacas for their meat between one to two years of age. This is known as culling the herd.

CARE

Alpacas can adapt to both very hot and very cold climates. They need at least a three-sided open shelter, if not a barn. That way, they can stay cool in summer and get out of the wind and snow in winter. The type of fencing used depends on the predators in the area. Possible predators include dogs, wolves, coyotes, and mountain lions.

Grass and hay are the alpaca's main diet. Unlike goats and sheep, which have long tongues that can rip plants out of the ground, alpacas have short tongues. They nibble only the tops of grasses and other plants. This results in less disturbance of

A baby alpaca is called a cria.

It is helpful to bind an alpaca's legs when it is being sheared so it doesn't move around and accidentally get hurt by the blades. The haircut does not take long and does not harm the animal.

the vegetation. Alpacas also need access to fresh water at all times. Each animal may drink at least 1 gallon (4 L) a day.

Alpacas have strong herd instincts. They need the companionship of other alpacas and should never be kept alone. Most of the time, female and male alpacas should be kept separately.

These animals don't need to be bathed. But they must be sheared once a year. This means cutting off their fleece. Shearing in the spring helps keep the alpacas cool in the summer. It also provides the owner with fleece.

BEES

There are two categories of bees that pollinate crops. These include honeybees and wild native bees. Farmers depend on them both.

For thousands of years, early civilizations collected honey and honeycomb from wild honeybee nests. Honeycomb is the group of small cells in which bees store their honey. Then people started making artificial hives for the bees. One of the earliest civilizations to keep bees this way was the ancient Egyptians. By 2450 BCE the Egyptians had developed horizontal hives made of dried mud and straw. They stacked the hives on top of each other. This method spread throughout the Mediterranean area. By 400 BCE the Greeks were using horizontal pottery hives. As beekeeping methods spread, most ancient cultures kept bees that were native to their regions.

There are more than 2.6 million honeybee colonies in the United States.

During the Middle Ages (500–1500 CE), honey and beeswax became important items for European trade. When Europeans began exploring, they took honeybees with them. In 1622,

English colonists brought honeybees to the Jamestown settlement in what is now Virginia. The honeybees thrived in the forests of North America and spread across the continent.

In the mid-1800s, people brought Italian honeybees to the United States. These honeybees had a calm nature and produced a lot of honey. They quickly became the most popular type of honeybee.

During the early 1900s, tractors and other machinery made it possible for farms to grow larger. Huge farms took over some

The United States has about 4,000 native bee species. The blue orchard bee is among those that people keep.

Inside the hive, bees store honey in honeycombs, which have six-sided compartments.

of the habitats of the wild native bees. Beekeepers put their bees in artificial hives and moved them around to pollinate crops for the farmers. Today beekeepers still take their bees to crop farms.

PURPOSE

There are six main products that come from honeybee hives. The most well-known product is honey. Honeybees make honey for food. They make more than they need, so beekeepers collect the excess. On average, a beekeeper can collect about 4.2 gallons (15.9 L) of honey each year from a healthy colony. Honey is used in food, lotions, and more.

Royal jelly has a milky appearance and is rich in protein.

The other products from bees are often used for medicinal and health purposes. Three of these products are beeswax, bee pollen, and royal jelly. Beeswax is made from honeycomb. Bee pollen is pollen mixed with nectar, honey, wax, and digestive enzymes from the bees. Royal jelly is a milky substance made by worker bees. It is used to feed the queen bee and larvae, or baby bees.

Two other products are propolis and bee venom. Propolis is a waxy substance that bees create by mixing their saliva with beeswax. Bees use it to seal gaps in the hive. It contains many vitamins and other nutrients. Bee venom comes from the stingers of bees. People use it to treat pain, illnesses, and many other medical conditions.

The most important role of bees is to serve as crop pollinators. More than 90 crops in the United States rely on bees for pollination. Approximately one-third of the food eaten by Americans comes from crops pollinated by honeybees and native wild bees.

Cherry blossoms need pollination to produce fruit.

CARE

Honeybees can be kept anywhere there are enough flowers growing. The location needs sunlight in the morning so the bees can warm up. Shade in the afternoon helps them cool off again. A source of fresh water should be nearby.

The honeybee hive should include vertical frames where the bees build honeycombs. When these become full of honey, the beekeeper must remove some honey or build more frames.

In human-made hives, bees make honeycomb on frames that can be easily removed so farmers can harvest the honey.

Bamboo or other hollow stems can be stacked together to make a native bee hotel. Solitary bees shelter in the hollow cavities.

Otherwise, the bees will swarm, meaning the older bees that make the most honey will leave to find a new place to start a hive.

Honeybees do not hibernate in the winter. In cold climates, they huddle around the queen bee to keep her warm. This means they need honey to eat in the winter. Beekeepers should leave enough honey in the hive for the bees.

Most native bees live alone. They are called solitary bees. Solitary bees make up about 98 percent of the native bee species in the United States. They make nests underground or in wooden tunnels. Farmers can provide nesting habitats in areas such as pastures or patches of soil. Many solitary bees stay near their nests, so they help pollinate the farm.

BISON

An adult bison weighs up to 2,000 pounds (910 kg).

Bison are large animals native to North America. Before European settlers arrived, bison roamed across most of the continent. In the early 1700s, settlers began domesticating and breeding some of the bison. As the settlers moved westward, they pushed the bison out west as well. By the early 1800s, there were no more wild bison in the East.

In the West, American Indian people relied on the bison for many things, including food, shelter, and clothing. But as the settlers moved into western territories, the bison began to disappear. White trappers and hunters killed millions of bison for their hides and for sport. Later, US Army troops killed even more bison to deprive American Indians of food. Before 1868, between 30 and 60 million bison roamed the Great Plains and the Midwest. Within 20 years, there were fewer than 1,000 bison left.

In the early 1900s, several ranchers gathered up the remaining bison. In doing so, they helped keep the bison from becoming extinct. Some bison were released into protected areas such as Yellowstone National Park. These herds helped re-establish the bison's wild populations. During the 1960s, ranchers began raising bison for meat.

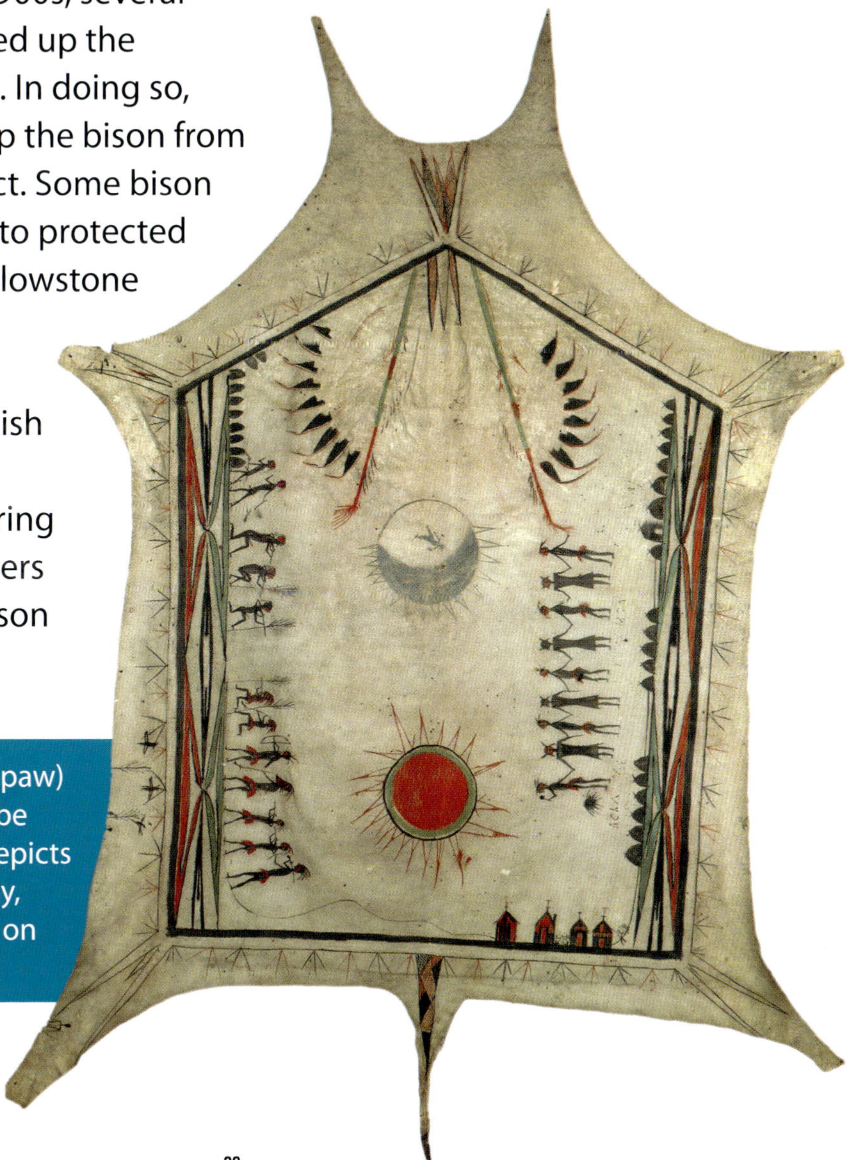

The Ogáxpa (Quapaw) Three Villages Robe from the 1700s depicts a battle, ceremony, and other scenes on a bison skin.

Today there are approximately 400,000 bison. About 20,000 bison are in American Indian herds, and approximately 30,000 are in wild herds. Farmers are raising 350,000 more.

PURPOSE

One of the main products that comes from bison is meat. Like beef, bison meat is a good source of protein. It also

A farmer needs at least 2 to 3 acres (0.8 to 1.2 ha) per female bison and calf in the herd.

Bison meat can be substituted for beef when making burgers.

provides many of the same nutrients, such as iron, zinc, vitamin B6, and vitamin B12. Bison meat can be eaten the same way as beef. It can be served as steak or ground up to make meals such as hamburgers, meatloaf, chili, and tacos.

Some people prefer to eat bison meat instead of beef. Bison meat is lower in calories and fat. And compared to most beef cattle, bison are raised more naturally on the open range, eating just hay and grass. But eating grass makes their fat yellow, and most people prefer the fat to be white. For this reason, they are usually given grain during the last 90 to 120 days before slaughter.

As with other livestock, bison calves may lose their mothers. Farmers must care for the calves, feeding them milk frequently.

Most meat sold comes from bison bulls between 18 and 36 months old. At this age, a bison weighs approximately 1,100 to 1,200 pounds (500 to 540 kg). The meat is sold to restaurants and individuals. Bison meat is available in specialty meat shops, in grocery stores, and directly from farmers.

Other products people buy are the heads and hides of bison. The heads are sold as mounted trophies. Bison skulls are cleaned and used as decoration. The hides are turned into leather.

CARE

Bison on farms are only partly domesticated. Farmers who raise bison must manage them as wild animals. After farmers put their herds in the pasture, the bison mostly take care of themselves.

A bison herd should have at least one bull and 10 to 15 cows. Raising bison is like raising beef cattle. However, bison are larger and stronger than cattle. Their larger size allows them to shove their way through almost all fencing that can contain other types of livestock. They can also jump fences up to 6 feet (1.8 m) high. For this reason, bison need special fencing and handling facilities.

Sturdy metal fencing can help keep bison contained.

Bison prefer land that has boulders, rocks, woods, and thickets. Their pasture should have a source of clean, fresh water, such as a river, stream, or pond. A herd of 15 animals may require up to 230 gallons (870 L) of water per day in the summer. If a bison's food and water requirements are met, it

Bison tend to move as they eat, so they are less likely than cattle to strip one part of a pasture of food.

Bison fur traps body heat to keep the animals warm in winter.

will stay within the fenced area. Otherwise the bison will probably escape.

Bison do not need an outside shelter, even in bad weather. Instead they turn to face storms. When it snows, they lie down and let the snow cover them. Farmers also do not have to worry about predators. Bison protect themselves. If a predator comes into the pasture, the herd will circle around it and drive it away.

CAMELS

Dromedary camel

There are two types of camels. Camels with one hump are dromedaries. They are found mostly in North Africa and the Middle East. Camels with two humps are called Bactrian camels. They live in the cold desert areas of northeast and central Asia. Camels can live in both hot and cold climates. They do well in temperature ranges from 20 to 120 degrees Fahrenheit (–7 to 49°C).

Dromedaries were first domesticated in Southern Arabia around 4000 to 3000 BCE. The camels carried people and goods across dry, hot regions. They also provided milk, meat, and hides.

Bactrian camel

At one time, all dromedaries were domesticated animals. But some escaped, and others were released back into the wild. Their descendants adapted to survive. These are known as feral dromedaries. They can be found in certain regions, such as parts of Australia and the Arabian Peninsula.

Bactrian camels were first domesticated around 4,500 years ago. They were used for carrying loads and producing wool. Nearly all of the 1.4 million Bactrian camels alive today are domesticated. Today fewer than 1,000 Bactrian camels live in the wild.

Camels can travel across the desert at the same speed as horses.

Camels were first brought to the United States by the US Army in 1856. The army planned to use them to carry supplies between remote military outposts. The camels could move more easily in the hot desert climate of the Southwest than mules or horses. They also required less food and water. But the Civil War (1861–1865) brought an end to the camel experiment. Some living

Zoos around the United States keep camels today. Sometimes people can pay to ride them.

When people have a lot of items to transport, they may tie many camels together single file in what is called a camel train or caravan.

in Southern states were set free by the South's Confederate Army. Others were eventually auctioned off. Some were sold to circuses or zoos. People saw wild camels in Arizona, New Mexico, and California until the 1930s.

PURPOSE

Today camels are an important farm animal in most of the dry areas of the world, especially Africa and the Middle East. They are still used for travel across dry regions. They can easily carry 200 pounds (90 kg) and travel about 20 miles (32 km) a day through the harsh desert.

A camel produces 1.3 to 1.6 gallons (5 to 6 L) of milk per day.

Camels are raised mostly for milk production. This is especially important in areas where there are long droughts. In these places, camel milk may supply to up to 50 percent of people's total nutrients. Kenya and Somalia are the world's leading producers of camel milk.

Camel milk does not have as much sugar as other milks, so it does not taste as sweet. It is rich in vitamins such as B1, B2, and C. It also has ten times the amount of iron as cow milk. The milk is available for as long as the baby, called a calf, is nursing. Calves usually nurse for 10 to 18 months.

In some countries, camels are also raised for their meat. Camel meat has less fat and cholesterol than many other livestock meats, such as beef. It is also high in protein and other nutrients.

People also collect the hair fibers from Bactrian camels. The hair is collected as the animal naturally sheds its coat. Each camel produces about 5 pounds (2.3 kg) of fiber per year. It is used mainly for overcoats, blankets, and rugs.

In Iran, people harvest hair from camels to make clothes, rugs, and more.

CARE

Camels should be kept in an area with enough space to roam and explore. They graze for about six to eight hours every day. They also browse, eating thorns and weeds that other animals leave behind. Browsing camels take only one or two bites from a plant. Then they move on to the next bush or tree.

Camels need strong fences with sturdy latches on the gates. The animals have split prehensile lips. This means they can use

Because food can be scarce in deserts, camels eat a wide variety of foods.

Camels need shelter to provide shade when it is more than 104 degrees Fahrenheit (40°C).

their lips to grasp things. They can open gate latches. Fencing also needs to protect the camels from predators. Wolves and big cats often attack sick or injured camels. Calves are most at risk.

Camels need shelter where they can get out of the wind, rain, and sun. The floor should be a dirt floor or covered in sand so the camels do not slip and injure themselves. Their bedding can be clean straw or sand.

Camels are social animals. They do best with other camels. The best groupings are all males, all females, or a single male with multiple females.

CATS

Cats use their senses of sight, smell, and hearing to catch prey.

Domesticated cats descended from the North African wildcat, also known as the Southwest Asian wildcat. Domestication began in the Middle Eastern region known as the Fertile Crescent about 8,000 years ago. When people farmed the land, they would store some of the grain. The grain was an easy food source for rodents such as rats and mice. Cats that were tolerant of humans began hunting the rodents near the farms. The farmers liked this because rodents damaged the food. Farmers provided the cats with food and shelter.

Rats and mice on ships were also a problem. They chewed through ropes and ate sailors' stored food. Sailors began bringing cats on their ships too. This allowed cats to relocate all around the world. Cats spread from Southwest Asia to Europe as early as 4400 BCE and to China by 3500 BCE. They had reached Cyprus by 2500 BCE. By 2000 BCE cats were in Egypt. During the time of the Roman Empire (27 BCE–476 CE), Egyptian cats expanded through the Mediterranean area, mixing with the cats in the Near East.

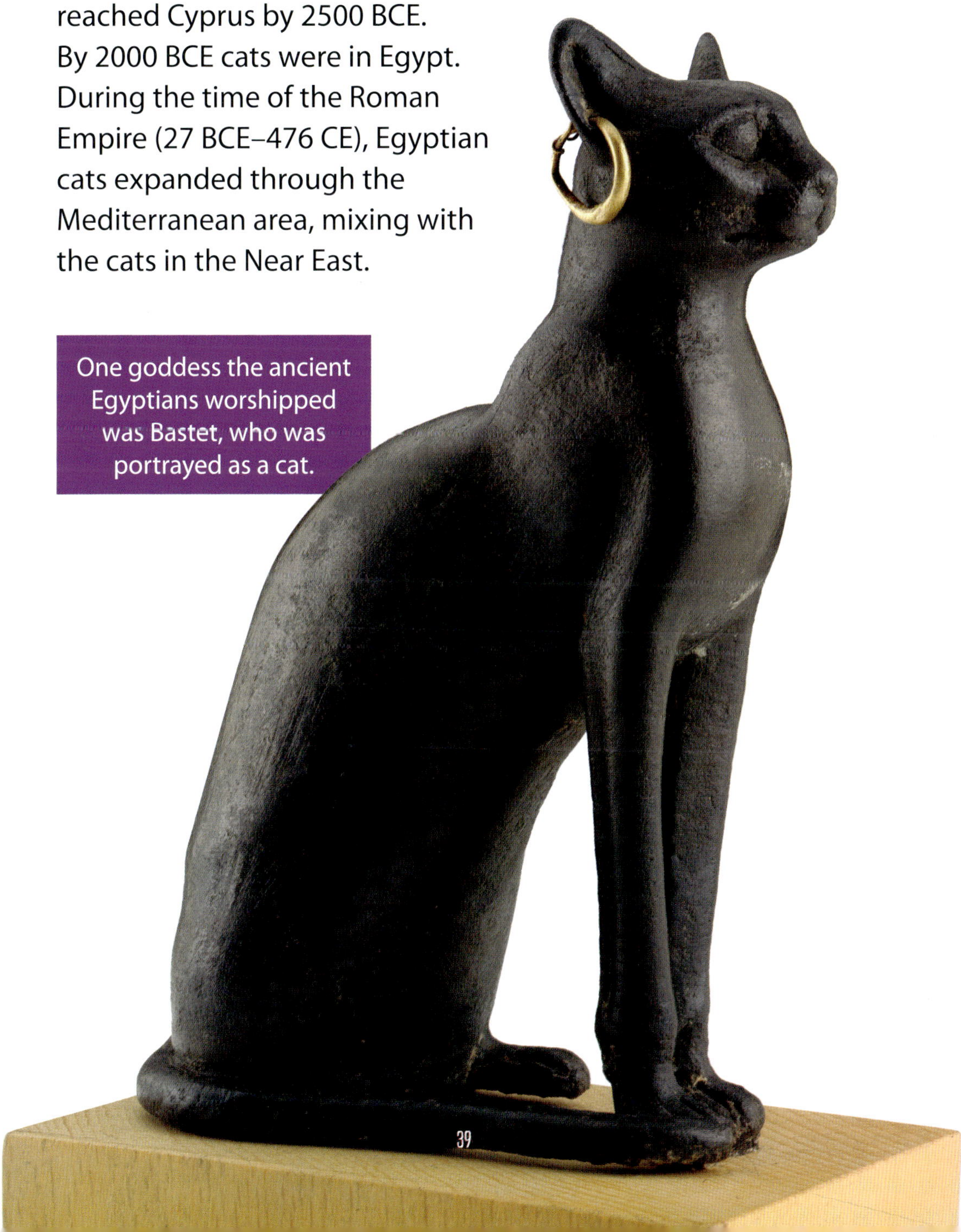

One goddess the ancient Egyptians worshipped was Bastet, who was portrayed as a cat.

European colonists and explorers traveled to the Americas starting in the 1400s. Cats went with them. By the end of the 1800s, cats were kept as pets all over the world.

PURPOSE

Farmers still use cats as pest control. Cats on a farm catch mice, rats, and other rodents. These animals are very

More than 46 million households had at least one pet cat in 2023.

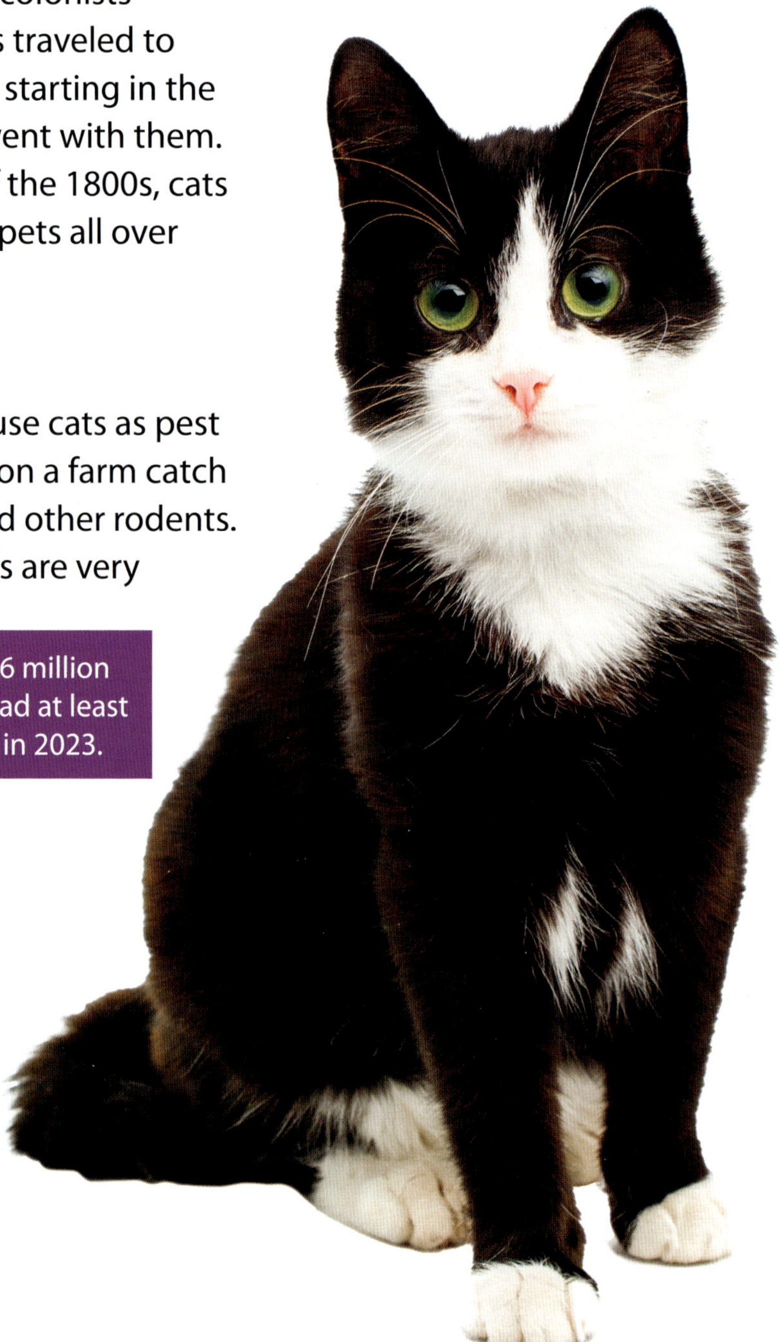

Rodents can spread a bacterial disease called leptospirosis, a viral disease called mpox, and other diseases.

destructive on a farm. Rodents eat and contaminate stored grains. They destroy 70 million tons (63 million metric tons) of rice, wheat, and maize every year. Rodents also dig up and eat the seeds farmers have planted. They leave droppings that contaminate animal feed and spread disease.

Rodents chew up a lot of things on a farm. They chew through plastic containers of seeds. They can chew through electrical wires, including car and tractor wires. This can lead to expensive repairs.

Barn cats hunt for mice among hay bales, which mice use as food and for nesting.

Some farmers may try using poison to get rid of the rodents. However, other animals or children may also get into the poison. Traps are another option, but these can be dangerous for other animals too. Instead, cats provide an effective, natural answer to the pest problem.

There are many breeds of cats. Purebred cats and house cats are usually kept only as companions. Cats working on the farm are often called barn cats. Barn cats are not always suited for indoor family life. Some may be friendly toward people, while others may hide from people. But they do their job well.

CARE

Even though barn cats live outside, they have the same basic needs as house cats. For example, barn cats need shelter where they can get out of hot, cold, or stormy weather. This is usually a barn or shed. It should contain an area where they can sleep and eat safely.

The Maine coon cat is a breed that was developed for its good mousing skills. These large cats can weigh up to 25 pounds (11 kg).

Barn cats also need to be fed a healthy diet. Even though they are catching rodents, they require additional food, especially when the weather is cold. A good quality cat food helps the cats keep up their energy. It is best to place the

Owners can use feeding time to help teach their barn cats to accept petting and interaction.

If barn cats do have kittens, they can need extra care, such as warmth if it is cold outside.

food on a high shelf so that wild animals are not attracted to it. When farmers feed their barn cats, they are helping teach the cat where home is.

Many farmers have their barn cats spayed or neutered. This means that they will not be able to have kittens. This is important because cats reproduce quickly. A female cat can have up to three litters of kittens a year. She may have up to six kittens in one litter, or up to 18 kittens in one year. When farmers need new barn cats, they often adopt them from an animal shelter instead. Many stray cats find new homes on farms as barn cats too.

CATTLE

Aurochs stood about 6 feet (1.8 m) tall at the shoulder.

Cattle were first domesticated in Southwest Asia about 10,000 years ago. Scientists believe they came from a type of wild cattle called aurochs. Aurochs were much bigger than modern cattle. Today aurochs are extinct, meaning there are none left in the world. But they once grazed and roamed in small herds.

After cattle were domesticated, Europeans brought them along as they moved and explored. In the early 1500s, Spanish explorers brought herds of cattle into the southern United States. Their breed of cattle became known as the Spanish longhorn.

In the early 1600s, colonists from Europe brought cattle with them for milk and meat. Durham cattle were introduced into the United States from England in the 1800s. These were known as shorthorns. They were larger and had more meat than the longhorns. People began crossbreeding the cattle. By the late 1800s, people began breeding cattle especially for dairy products. At the same time, Angus and Hereford cattle were being bred for beef.

The early 1900s saw many people in the United States and Europe moving from farms to find work in the cities. They had to start buying milk. New inventions helped mass produce it. These included milking machines and pasteurization equipment.

Today's Texas longhorn is descended from the Spanish longhorn.

Angus cattle are typically black.

By 1947 people in the United States were eating much more beef. Instead of waiting until the cattle were fully grown, beef producers began processing them sooner. American farmers brought in other breeds from Europe and crossbred them to increase their size.

PURPOSE

Cattle are raised mainly for their dairy and meat products. Female cattle that have had calves are called cows. Cow milk is used to make products such as cheese, butter, yogurt, and ice cream. One of the most popular breeds of dairy cow is the Holstein.

When cows give birth to calves, the mothers produce milk. Dairy cows are bred to produce more milk than their calves will drink. One dairy cow can produce 6 gallons (23 L) of milk a day. On large commercial dairy farms, the calves are separated from their mothers. Female calves can grow to become breeders or milk producers. But most male calves are not needed. These calves are raised until they are about 16 to 18 weeks old. Then they are slaughtered. The meat is known as veal.

The Holstein is usually black and white. About 90 percent of dairy cows in the United States are Holsteins.

Beef cattle are bred to grow quickly and be very muscular. The most common breed in the United States is the Angus. Beef cattle are usually slaughtered between 18 and 24 months old. The meat of these young cattle is more tender and flavorful than that of older cattle.

Female beef cattle with desirable traits become breeders. These traits include an easygoing temperament, resistance to disease, and good mothering ability. The females give birth to one calf each year. They have their last calf when they are about nine years old. Then the cows go to the beef market. As older cows, they often become inexpensive ground beef.

CARE

Cattle do best in herds on grasslands. This is called pasture-based farming. In the pasture, cattle need access to trees or a shelter for shade. Fencing should include electric wire since cattle can easily push through a fence.

Steak and cheese are among the popular products from cattle.

Tracking a calf's growth by weighing it or measuring its height can help farmers make sure a calf is healthy.

Feedlots typically add food to cattle troughs more than once a day.

Cattle eat up to 26 pounds (12 kg) of food per day. Their natural diet consists of mainly grasses, legumes, alfalfa, and clover. In the winter, cows still eat grass in the form of hay. Farmers may also give their cows other feed such as corn or soybeans.

Some beef cattle are taken to feedlots about three to five months before they are slaughtered. A feedlot is a confined area or building where the cattle are fattened up. This is called finishing. The cattle do not have to forage. Instead, high-protein food is brought to them. Sometimes calves are also raised in feedlots.

When producing milk, dairy cows can drink 50 gallons (190 L) of water a day. If dairy cows get too hot, milk production

goes down. So, many dairy farmers use fans and sprinklers or mister systems in their barns. Water affects how much beef cattle eat. If there is not enough water, or the water is poor quality, the cattle will not eat as much. The cattle will produce less meat.

On many farms, human workers attach the milker to the cow. But some farms have robotic milkers that use sensors to attach the milker.

CHICKENS

India has a large population of red junglefowl. Males, *right*, are more colorful than females, *left*.

The Southeast Asian red junglefowl is the primary wild ancestor of chickens. Evidence of domesticated chickens dates back to at least 3000 BCE. These chickens were probably used for cockfighting. Cockfighting is a sport where two trained roosters are brought together to fight each other. The birds are usually injured, and sometimes they die.

Chickens arrived in ancient Egypt as fighting birds around 1750 BCE. After about 1,000 years, the Egyptians began using chickens as a source of food. They built large structures for incubating the eggs with heat from fires. Because the hens were not sitting on the eggs, they could continue laying.

Cockfighting spread throughout Asia and the Middle East and into Europe. People from all economic statuses enjoyed it,

including the ancient Romans. The Romans began eating chickens as a delicacy. They experimented with different breeds and types of feed to get bigger birds. The Romans also ate the eggs. They are credited with inventing the omelet.

A Roman mosaic from about 2,000 years ago shows chickens, *bottom left*, among other foods.

Polynesians likely brought the first chickens to the Americas in the 1300s. These birds were used for cockfighting and for food. Europeans also brought chickens. As Americans selected chickens for specific physical traits, they developed new breeds. By the late 1800s, many households had backyard flocks for supplying eggs or meat.

During the 1920s and 1930s, Americans began raising chickens specifically for their meat. These chickens became known as broilers. Commercial chicken farms grew, and by 1952 broilers surpassed farm chickens as the main source of chicken meat in the United States. In 1985 Americans were eating more chicken than pork. By 1992 more people were eating chicken than beef.

Chicken breasts have a mild flavor, so a variety of seasonings pair well with them.

Broiler chickens grow larger and more quickly than other types of chickens.

PURPOSE

Chickens provide meat and eggs, two important food products. These birds are raised for meat all over the world. In the United States, almost all chicken meat comes from broilers. Broiler chickens are usually slaughtered before they are two months old. The United States produces the most chicken, followed by China and Brazil. This is partly because the United States also grows large amounts of the crops used in chicken feed, including soybean meal and corn.

Plymouth Rock chicken

Rhode Island red chicken

People also raise chickens for the eggs they produce. Chickens begin laying when they are around four to five months old. Once hens reach laying age, they lay about one egg per day. However, they usually slow down or stop egg production during the fall and winter. Hens continue laying until they are about three to four years old. The United States has more than 300 million hens. Each one lays an average of 300 eggs a year.

On a commercial farm, some chickens are breeder hens. These are birds that lay eggs for hatching. There are more than 1,600 different chicken breeds. Some breeds are raised for meat, such as the fast-growing Cornish, New Hampshire, and Plymouth Rock breeds. Popular egg-laying breeds include Rhode Island reds and Ameraucanas.

CARE

Chickens are social animals. Farmers should have a flock of at least three birds. But no matter how many birds there are, chickens need a coop to keep them safe. Many different animals kill chickens, especially at night. These include dogs, foxes, coyotes, raccoons, bobcats, snakes, and skunks.

In the coops, chickens need perches. Perches let chickens sleep high off the ground. This keeps them safer from predators.

A chicken coop should be secure against all the potential predators in the area.

A nesting box should be about 12 inches (30 cm) tall, wide, and deep.

Farmers add nesting boxes to the coop to encourage the hens to lay their eggs in a safe place for collecting or hatching. Three to five birds can share one nesting box.

Some farmers raise free-range chickens. This means the chickens can go outside of their pen for all or part of the day. They may be in a backyard, a pasture, or an open field. Free-range chickens eat insects, weeds, and plants. Other farmers feed their chickens grain or other chicken feed. This is especially true on large or commercial farms where the chickens do not have free range.

Chicken feed often includes ingredients such as barley, corn, animal fat, canola, and more.

DOGS

For thousands of years, people have used dogs to track game when hunting.

Many scientists believe dogs were the first domesticated animals. Dogs domesticated themselves. They descended from wolves. Most wolves were fearful of and aggressive toward humans. But some wolves moved near human camps to look for leftover food. People likely killed the more aggressive wolves. They let the friendlier wolves stay nearby.

The wolves that stayed near humans eventually changed in physical appearance. They began to look more like the dogs of today. As people turned from hunting to agriculture, they began moving to new areas. Farmers from places around the Mediterranean Sea migrated to western Asia and Europe. Their dogs went with them.

By 5000 BCE dogs could be found everywhere. Dogs took on many different jobs. They helped humans track prey when they hunted. Dogs also pulled sleds for transportation, and they warned people of danger by barking. They herded livestock such as sheep and cattle. They protected the livestock from predators. They helped keep away pests by catching rats and mice.

The Border collie is one of the most skilled herding breeds. People continue to breed this dog for its ability to move livestock.

People began breeding dogs that could fill these roles. They bred the dogs with the traits they wanted. For example, the ancient Romans bred white dogs to help protect sheep. The white dogs would not be mistaken for wolves at night. Other farm dogs were black to be less visible to nighttime trespassers. The Romans also bred dogs to have stronger natural instincts for certain jobs, such as keeping animals together or protecting them from intruders.

Livestock guardian dogs do not usually have to fight predators. Their size and bark scare away most threats.

The Kangal dog is an LGD from Turkey.

Today dogs are still fulfilling these roles on farms. People have continued to breed them for many useful traits and skills. Dogs also provide companionship for many farm families.

PURPOSE

Farm dogs help keep the farm running smoothly. They keep watch over the farm. They bark to announce when visitors arrive.

Some farm dogs protect herds of livestock, keeping them safe from predators. The dogs stay with the livestock all the time. Great Pyrenees and Anatolian shepherds are popular livestock guardian dogs (LGDs). They bond with the group of animals they are protecting. Their large size and heavy coats make it easy for them to live outdoors.

Some dogs are herders. Herding dogs include Border collies, Australian shepherds, and Australian cattle dogs. These dogs move groups of livestock from one place to another. They use their natural instincts to control and direct animals.

Other dogs are good at controlling pests. These include breeds of terriers, such as Russell terriers and Patterdale terriers. They keep rodents, raccoons, and other wildlife away from the farm.

People are finding new ways to use farm dogs too. Some dogs use their strong sense of smell to find invasive weeds. These weeds do not naturally grow in the area and can threaten crops and the environment. Some dogs can detect certain

The Australian cattle dog was developed in Australia in the 1800s. It originally herded wild cattle.

diseases in plants, while others sniff out valuable mushrooms called truffles.

CARE

The choice of LGD breed depends on a farmer's situation and needs. Shorthaired LGDs do better in hot climates, and longhaired LGDs do better in cold places. Farmers in areas with large predators such as bears or mountain lions will need larger dogs than farmers who live where the main predators are coyotes. If there are a lot of livestock, more than one guard dog is required.

Most Patterdale terriers still work controlling pests. They have a lot of energy and a strong hunting instinct.

Training helps teach a dog to take direction from the owner and to accept handling.

Many farm dogs live inside the house with their owners. But LGDs must stay with the livestock. They need strong fencing or electric fencing. An informational sign is also a good idea. It lets people know the dog is on duty and has not been abandoned.

No matter their roles, farm dogs need to be trained so they can perform their duties.

For example, herding dogs must learn how to direct livestock both independently and by responding to the owner's cues. LGDs must bond with the sheep as puppies while still obeying their owners.

Dogs have natural predatory instincts. These help some dogs do their jobs, such as getting rid of rodents and other pests. However, for other farm dogs, it is important to stop these behaviors. Otherwise they may harm other animals on the farm.

Farmers might let their chickens graze across the property during the day. Farm dogs need to leave the chickens alone.

DONKEYS

African wild asses have black stripes on their legs and a dark stripe down the back.

In about 5000 BCE, donkeys were first domesticated from wild asses in eastern Africa. Their use spread quickly. Donkeys have a lot of endurance, and they can carry heavy loads. They can transport large amounts of goods and supplies over long distances and across difficult terrain.

During the Bronze Age (3000–1000 BCE), people began working with metal. They mixed tin and copper to make bronze, which was harder and more durable than copper or tin alone. It was a good metal for making tools and weapons. This increased the demand for donkeys. They could carry heavy loads of metal over long distances to areas that didn't have much metal naturally, such as ancient Mesopotamia.

Ancient Mesopotamia was located in what is now western Asia. The people of Mesopotamia also had stocky, horse-like animals called kungas. These were a cross between female donkeys and male Syrian wild asses. They combined the strength and speed of the wild asses with the tame temperament of domesticated donkeys. Kungas also pulled wheeled vehicles into battle.

A donkey can safely carry up to 30 percent of its weight.

The ancient Romans also crossbred donkeys. They needed a way to transport military equipment and goods. Between 300 and 600 BCE, they bred African donkeys with horses to produce mules. Like kungas, mules could carry heavy loads. Mules also pulled heavy catapults for the Roman army. They became the most important working animals for the Roman military.

Over the next 2,500 years, domesticated donkeys spread throughout Europe and Asia. These developed into the donkeys found today. In many communities in Africa and the Middle East, people still rely on donkeys to carry people and goods.

Donkeys crossed with draft horses have draft mule offspring. Mules have larger ears than horses do.

Guard donkeys can be kept in pairs so they have the company of at least one other donkey.

PURPOSE

Donkeys serve many roles on farms. One of these jobs is serving as guardians for other farm animals. Donkeys have very good hearing and a wider field of vision than horses. They defend their pasture against predators such as foxes, dogs, and coyotes by chasing them away. Donkeys often use their teeth and hooves to bite or kick a predator. They may bray very loudly. Afterward the donkey needs time to calm down.

Small donkeys should be ridden only by children. But larger donkeys can be ridden by adults.

Donkeys are also load carriers. They can transport heavy loads of feed, water, and equipment around the farm. Their strong backs and sure-footedness help them cross uneven terrain. This makes them the ideal choice for reaching remote or challenging areas. Donkeys can also carry children on their backs. Well-trained donkeys can make good riding animals for young children who are just starting to learn.

In some places, donkeys are used for light plowing. They can pull plows and other small farm tools to help prepare the soil for planting. They can pull carts with supplies.

Donkeys also provide companionship to other farm animals, especially horses and ponies. This companionship can reduce stress and anxiety among the animals. Horses often become less nervous with a donkey around.

CARE

A donkey needs at least 0.5 acres (0.2 ha) of land to roam and graze. That way, it has enough room to exercise and enough access to fresh forage. One acre (0.4 ha) of land is enough for the donkey to have a companion.

Donkeys and horses can get along, but they both have their own needs that must be met.

Donkeys can gain weight easily, which can lead to health issues. The best diet for a donkey is clean straw. Barley straw is one of the best choices. During warmer months, donkeys can graze in the pasture. In the winter when grass is scarce, a diet of straw and hay is enough.

Donkeys need a sturdy structure, barn, or lean-to for shelter. Unlike horses, donkeys' coats do not get much thicker in winter. They are not able to regulate their body heat as well when it gets cold. Donkeys will look for shelter when the temperature falls below 57 degrees Fahrenheit (14°C).

A three-sided shelter can protect donkeys from wind, rain, and snow.

Training should begin when a donkey is a foal.

A donkey's hooves need to be trimmed every six to ten weeks. If the hooves become overgrown, the donkey's feet can become sore, and it may not be able to walk well. The donkey should be trained to stand still and allow its feet to be handled.

DUCKS

Male and female Muscovy ducks have red wattles, or extra skin, around the face.

Almost all domesticated ducks today are descended from a wild species called the mallard. These wild ducks live in Europe, Asia, North Africa, and North America. The Egyptians, Chinese, and Europeans began domesticating ducks by 4000 BCE. In Central and South America, people domesticated Muscovy ducks. This is the only domesticated duck species that did not come from the mallard.

Wild mallards are native to the United States. During the 1600s, the ducks could be found all along the east coast of North America. Settlers also began raising ducks on their farms. They either domesticated the ducks in North America or brought them over from Europe.

Raising ducks commercially in the United States began on Long Island, New York, in 1873. That year, a few Pekin ducks were brought from China. Duck farmers came to prefer the Pekin duck over other breeds. Pekins needed only 10 to 12 weeks to grow big enough to sell. Other commercial ducks took 20 to 24 weeks to grow large enough. Pekin duck meat was tender and juicy.

Pekin ducks are white with orange or yellow beaks and legs.

Commercial duck farms need to keep the bedding in the barns clean and dry.

Farms started up all over the island. By the 1960s, approximately 7.5 million ducks were being raised there. People began using the term Long Island Duck to refer to ducks sold to restaurants and grocery stores.

Eventually most Long Island farms closed because of city growth and concerns for the environment. Ducks continued to be raised elsewhere. Today more than 30 million ducks are raised on commercial farms in the United States each year. However, China leads in duck production. It produces approximately 65 percent of the duck meat worldwide.

PURPOSE

There are many breeds of ducks. Some breeds are better for meat production. These include the Pekin and Muscovy. However, duck meat is usually harder to collect than chicken meat. A duck's feathers are more firmly rooted than those of a chicken. They also do not have as much meat on the thighs as chickens.

Duck meat has more flavor than chicken meat. It is also more tender.

Some ducks are better for egg production. While ducks do not lay eggs every day, they continue to lay through the winter. Good egg-laying breeds include the Khaki Campbell, Silver Appleyard, and Welsh harlequin. A single duck from these breeds can produce approximately 250 to 325 eggs a year. Ducks can continue to lay at this rate until they are about four to five years old. Most stop laying when they are seven to nine years old.

Some people who cannot digest chicken eggs can eat duck eggs. This is because duck eggs have slightly different proteins. Duck eggs also have thicker shells. The thickness protects the eggs against wet conditions. It also helps them withstand rougher handling.

All ducks look through the dirt and mud for larvae, worms, and slugs. But some ducks are very good at keeping lawns and gardens free of insects and weeds. The Dutch hookbill and Indian runner ducks eat the insects, while the Ancona and magpie clear out the weeds.

Adele Campbell developed the Khaki Campbell in the late 1800s. She crossed Indian runners, a Rouen duck, and penciled runners.

Indian runner ducks have a naturally tall stance. They are more active than many other duck breeds.

CARE

Ducks do not have teeth to grind their food. Farmers provide them with finely crushed stone or sand called grit. Ducks eat the grit with their food. The grit helps them digest their food properly.

Ducks need access to water. While they don't necessarily require a pond, they do need water for drinking and bathing. A container such as a kiddie pool, water trough, or tub is enough. A week-old duckling drinks about 0.5 gallons (1.9 L) of water in

People can install artificial ponds for their ducks. These ponds need to be cleaned weekly.

Ducklings are usually a bit larger than chicks when they hatch. They also grow more quickly.

a week. By seven weeks old, it drinks approximately 0.5 gallons (1.9 L) of water a day.

Ducks are very adaptable to their environment. They often enjoy being in the rain and snow. However, farmers must make sure their ducks have shelter when they need it. Ducks also need a safe place to hide from predators such as foxes, raccoons, and birds of prey. Since ducks do not perch like chickens, they need straw bedding inside the shelter. This bedding will give them a comfortable place to rest.

FISH

Fish farming is also known as aquaculture. Aquaculture dates back thousands of years. People began keeping fish in ancient China by at least 1100 BCE. During the Zhou dynasty, people farmed fish called carp. They were considered symbols of good luck and fortune.

In Europe, aquaculture first began in ancient Rome. The Romans would catch fish in the ocean. Then they put the fish in pools until it was time to eat them.

Carp grow to about 12 to 25 inches (30 to 64 cm) in length.

Concarneau, France, had an aquaculture facility in the mid-1800s.

Wealthy people built pools inside their homes. Guests could then choose the fish they wanted to eat. During the Middle Ages in Europe, the upper class had similar fishponds.

New ways of fish farming were developed during the Renaissance (1300s–1600s CE). People wrote essays describing how ponds should be built. They discussed the types of fish to farm, as well as fish health and diet. Carp were popular in eastern Europe, and people built artificial ponds for them.

Hatcheries provide a safe place for fish to grow where few or no predators can reach them.

During the 1800s, the growth of industry created a lot of pollution. This caused a decrease in fish populations in Europe. Dams and canals disrupted the migration of certain fish such as salmon. To fix this problem, scientists figured out how to breed fish, move the eggs, and grow the fish in artificial ponds. Then they released the fish into the wild. This led to the opening of hatcheries all over the Western world. In the United States, commercial fish farming began in 1853 with the production of the freshwater rainbow trout.

Around the late 1950s, there was another big breakthrough in fish farming. People invented fish food that came in tiny grains. This led to large-scale commercial trout farming in the western United States.

Today aquaculture is the fastest-growing farming sector in the United States. In 2018 the number of fish raised on farms became greater than the number of fish caught in the wild.

Farmed fish of similar size are kept together while growing. They start in a nursery pond. As they grow, they move to bigger ponds.

Eating salmon has many health benefits, including keeping the brain and heart healthy.

PURPOSE

Aquaculture plays an important part in people's food supply. More than 100 fish species are farmed today. Although many fish can survive in a range of temperatures, some grow better in warm or cool water. Warm water species commonly farmed include tilapia, carp, and largemouth bass. Cool water species include salmon, trout, and perch.

Fish farming helps threatened and endangered fish species. Farmers breed and raise these fish in controlled environments. This helps prevent overfishing of the species in the wild.

Besides providing seafood, aquaculture also contributes to education and recreation. Some of the fish raised in captivity go to places like zoos and aquariums. They are used to educate people about aquatic life. Some fish stock state waters. This allows more people to enjoy recreational fishing without causing a species to go extinct. Some fish are raised as bait for catching bigger fish.

Marine fish can be kept in ring cages in the ocean. The cages need to be able to withstand powerful ocean waves and currents.

Fish farmers use sensors to detect and monitor water quality in their tanks.

CARE

Fish farms should be located near a reliable source of water. The water should be free from pollution or chemicals. It is important that conditions such as water temperature and oxygen levels are just right for the type of fish the farmer is raising.

When it comes time to catch the fish, there are several different ways to do it. The method depends on the type of fish and how the farm is set up. Methods include using nets or traps. Traps are often made of wire or wood. The trap is baited. The fish can go in to get the bait, but they cannot come out again.

Farmed fish are usually fed pellets. These are made from a mix of fish oil, plants, and smaller fish. The pellets contain about 40 essential nutrients needed by the fish. Not all fish eat the same thing, so the pellets must have the right balance of nutrients for each particular species. That way, the fish can grow and stay healthy.

Fish need to be measured periodically to check their growth. Their size determines how much they are fed.

GEESE

Geese can have a variety of feather colors, including gray.

People have been raising geese since Egypt's New Kingdom period (1539–1075 BCE). The ancient Romans raised several varieties of geese. They bred the birds for specific traits, such as calm personalities or luxurious feathers. The feathers were used in cushions and upholstery, and the quills were used for writing. People also raised geese for their meat and eggs.

The European domesticated goose descended from the wild greylag goose. At first, wild geese were hunted. Later, people began raising them in flocks. Goslings, or baby geese, were easy to tame. The geese were fattened up, and eventually the wild geese became too heavy to fly well. In Southeast Asia, domesticated geese came from a different species, the swan goose. Today this domesticated goose is called the Chinese goose.

Europeans raised geese for hundreds of years. Geese were first brought to North America by European settlers. Eventually several breeds developed. These included the cotton patch, the pilgrim, and the American buff. The cotton patch was an important part of cotton production in the South. This goose ate weeds in cotton fields before herbicides were developed.

Today goose production is also important in Egypt, Poland, and Hungary. But it is most popular in China, which raises about 90 percent of the world's domestic geese.

Modern herbicides mean farmers no longer have to use geese to remove weeds from fields.

Geese spend most of their lives on land.

PURPOSE

Most goose breeds were developed for their meat. These include Embden geese, Toulouse geese, and African geese. Goose meat is rich and juicy without being greasy. Farmers begin preparing the goose for slaughter when it has grown all its feathers but is still younger than ten months old. This process is known as finishing. During the final three to five weeks, the geese are confined to an area where they cannot roam. The farmer then begins to fatten them up to make the meat taste better.

Geese also produce eggs. A goose egg is nearly three times the size of a chicken egg. They may be eaten, used for crafting, or incubated to hatch more geese. Females typically lay eggs during the spring into summer. Once they start, most lay an egg a day. Geese lay between 30 to 50 eggs in a year.

Geese typically begin laying eggs at nine months old.

Down and other feathers are another product geese provide. Down refers to a fluffy layer of feathers below the outer layer. These feathers are used for clothing and household items such as comforters and cushions. Farmers usually harvest goose down after the birds are slaughtered for meat.

Geese are also helpful around the farm. Because geese are territorial, they watch for intruders. They have better eyesight and hearing than humans. They will sound the alarm with loud honks if an animal

Geese bite with their serrated beaks.

Geese fight using their wings and beaks.

or person approaches. Geese are also good weeders for the garden. They will eat grasses and weeds and leave the garden plants alone.

CARE

A farmer can have anywhere from one goose to a large flock of geese. A flock of geese should have only one male. Otherwise the male geese may fight. A male goose will mate and bond for life with one or more females.

Geese spend about half their day eating.

Sometimes farmers will hand-raise their geese without the parents. When this happens, the geese often form a special bond with their humans. They may think of their people as part of their flock.

One acre (0.4 ha) of pasture will typically support a flock of 20 to 40 geese. By the time geese are five to six weeks old, they can get most of their diet

from the pasture. Besides plants, they also eat insects, snails, and worms. Some farmers feed their geese manufactured food. Geese need water to help them swallow their food and to prevent choking.

Geese do not need water for swimming, but they are happy if it is provided. A pond or pool works well. Regular bathing keeps their feathers in a healthy condition.

Large commercial farms raise geese in confinement. This allows for better control of the environment. Geese raised on these farms usually gain weight very quickly.

Geese lead their newly hatched young to water in order to teach them how to swim.

GOATS

Scientists believe goats were domesticated around 9000 to 8000 BCE in the Fertile Crescent. Domesticated goats descended mainly from the wild goat, whose scientific name is *Capra aegagrus*. The wild goat still lives in the mountains of Turkey, Iran, Pakistan, and the region called the Caucasus in southern Russia, Georgia, Armenia, and Azerbaijan.

Both male and female goats have horns.

Communities gradually started herding the goats. Then they began breeding them to their needs and preferences. The goats' social nature and adaptability made it easy for early civilizations to tame them.

When explorers and settlers began traveling by sea, they took goats with them. Soon goats were spreading around the world. African and Spanish goats went to the American colonies. Goats from Britain and Africa went to New Zealand,

Australia, and the Pacific islands. Goats successfully adapted to climates where other livestock would not do well, including deserts, mountains, and tropical areas.

Farmers can keep around six to eight goats per acre (0.4 ha) of land.

Many breeds began to develop in Europe and North America over the last 250 years. Angora goats are known for their fine hair. These goats were first developed in Turkey and came to the United States in the late 1800s.

In the early 1900s, dairy goats were also imported to the United States. In 1904 the first US dairy goat show was held at the Saint Louis World's Fair. After that, both Angora and dairy goats became very popular. Meat goats from South Africa and New Zealand arrived in the late 1900s. Today there are more than 200 breeds of goats.

Angora goats' hair can grow over their eyes if not cut.

Goat cheese tends to be softer than cheese made of cow milk.

PURPOSE

Goats provide people with many products and services. One of their main roles is the production of milk. These goats are called dairy goats. Popular dairy goat breeds include Nubian and Alpine goats.

Goat milk is rich in nutrients. Goat milk also has less lactose compared to cow milk. People who do not digest lactose well often prefer it to cow milk. The milk can be used to make a wide range of dairy products. These include cheese and yogurt. Soap and lotions are also made from the milk.

Farmers can use shears or electric clippers to remove hair from goats.

Goats are also a source of meat. Goat meat is higher in iron than beef, pork, lamb, or chicken. Goats are a valuable food source in many parts of the world. Meat goat breeds include La Mancha and Boer goats.

Some goats produce valuable fiber. Breeds such as Angora and cashmere goats have fine, soft fibers in their coats. These are used to make luxurious fabrics, including mohair and cashmere. These textiles are prized for their warmth and softness.

Another practical role of goats is in brush and weed control. Goats browse on overgrown vegetation. This helps maintain fields and pastures.

Goats also serve as companions for other farm animals. They provide social interaction and comfort to animals such as horses and sheep that can't live alone. However, they are happiest when they are with other goats.

Goats can become depressed if separated from other animals.

CARE

On the farm, goats get much of their food from the pasture. Farmers may also add hay and grain to their diets. Goats should have access to a shed or a small barn. This shelter protects them from harsh weather and provides a safe place to rest and sleep. The main predators of goats include dogs and coyotes.

Goats are known for getting through fences. Because goats are curious, they will test a fence and try to jump over it. Farmers should choose a type of fencing that is at least

It is best to keep goats out of the rain because wet hair does not hold heat as well as dry hair.

One reason goats like to climb things is that it makes them feel safe from predators.

4 feet (1.2 m) tall. This will prevent the goats from going over the top of it. It should also have openings no bigger than 4 inches (10 cm). Otherwise a goat might get its head stuck.

Keeping goats entertained will also help keep them in the pen. Goats enjoy climbing on things like rocks and old tires. Goats are herd animals, so they are happiest with other goats. Having company also helps make them less likely to test the fencing.

HORSES

Horses are among the smartest animals.

The early ancestors of horses lived in Europe and Asia. Some lived in the northern Caucasus region. People domesticated some of the horses in the Caucasus. They bred them to have stronger backs and a greater tolerance for stress. They used the horses for farming, transportation, and warfare. In about 2000 BCE, these horses spread across Europe and Asia.

As civilizations advanced, horses played an important role. People began to prefer horses over oxen for hauling goods and plowing fields. Horses could move much more quickly. In the United States, early settlers used horses to clear the land as they expanded their settlements.

Horses were also used for transportation, to pull plows, and to work with cattle. In the 1800s, cowboys in the western United States used horses to round up livestock. They often rode American quarter horses. South American ranch hands rode a breed called Criollos.

The unit *horsepower* was invented to compare the power of engines to that of draft horses.

By the beginning of the 1900s, most farmers relied on horses. Large draft horses did much of the hard work required to run their farms. These included Belgians, Clydesdales, Percherons, and Shires. By 1920 there were more than 25 million horses and mules in the United States. Most of them were working on farms.

The Great Depression (1929–1939) would change that, however. In 1929 the US economy crashed. Many people lost their jobs. In the years that followed, horses were sold off because people needed money. Also during this time, tractors and other modern farm equipment began replacing horses. One tractor could do the work of five horses.

The Shire is one of the largest horse breeds in the world. It can weigh up to 2,200 pounds (1,000 kg).

Ranchers may use horses to separate one cow from the herd to give it medical care.

Today there are more than 300 different breeds of horses. Some of these still plow fields. Some are still used to manage cattle. But many are kept for riding and as pets.

PURPOSE

Even with modern machinery, horses still play important roles on the farm. Some work as draft animals. They pull logs and haul heavy equipment. This reduces the need for fuel-powered machinery. Since horses need only grass and crops for food, they are more sustainable than vehicles that run on fuel.

Owners can train their draft horses to respond to directions while a person walks behind them. This skill is useful when pulling a plow or wagon.

Some farmers still use horses to plow fields. Horses are not as heavy as tractors. They do not compact the soil when they walk over it like tractors do. Plants do not grow as well in compacted soil. However, it takes much longer to plow with horses.

Some horses work with ranchers to move and manage cattle across large amounts of land. A ranch horse often has to carry a rancher long distances over difficult ground. For this reason, the horse must be easy to handle and have a lot of endurance. It must also be trustworthy. This helps ensure the rancher and livestock stay safe.

Horses also provide companionship. They may be companions for other livestock. They also serve as companions for the ranchers and farmers. Horses often form a special bond with their owners. This bond can help the owner feel calmer and happier.

CARE

Like some other farm animals, horses need access to a stable, shed, or other shelter. That way they can get out of harsh weather conditions such as wind or storms. Horses grow a thick coat to help them stay warm in the winter.

Individual horses in a herd can be more closely bonded with some herd members than others.

Horses require a consistent source of nutrition. Because they are grazing animals, they should have access to hay or pasture throughout the day. However, some horses require additional grain. Growing horses and horses that do heavy work need the extra energy.

Horses also need plenty of fresh water. Most 1,000-pound (450 kg) horses need 10 to 12 gallons (38 to 45 L) of water every day. They need more water in the winter when their food is drier.

Horses can eat 1.5 to 2 percent of their body weight in food every day.

Hoof dressing helps keep hooves from cracking.

Regular exercise is important for horse health. This can include riding and lunging. When a horse is lunging, it moves in a controlled circle at the end of a long line. This form of exercise helps the horse build muscle and focus its attention.

A horse's hooves also need care. They should be trimmed every six to eight weeks. This prevents them from getting too long, which causes the horse to limp. When its hooves are properly trimmed, the horse can move comfortably and avoid injuries.

LLAMAS

Llamas belong to the same family as alpacas and camels. Llamas descended from wild animals called guanacos. These animals roam South America's Andes mountains in Peru, Chile, Argentina, and Bolivia.

Guanacos live at high altitudes on rough terrain. Ancient people prized their meat, fine wool, and thick hides. They brought guanacos to lower altitudes and domesticated them around 4000 BCE. These guanacos developed into the llama.

Llamas were useful to the ancient herders in the Andes. They can carry up to 100 pounds (45 kg). Their nimble feet allow them to cross difficult areas with heavy loads.

Llamas can grow to a height of 6 feet (1.8 m).

Because of llamas, an Andean civilization known as the Inca was able to build a complex society connected by mountain roads. The Inca also used llamas for their fur and meat. Even their manure was used for fuel and fertilizer.

But the arrival of the Spanish in the 1500s CE marked a sharp decline in the number of llamas. Their population dropped by 90 percent as the Spanish conquered the Inca. Large numbers of llamas died because of the popularity of their meat and because of new European diseases. The Spanish also brought in sheep, which competed with llamas for grazing land.

Machu Picchu is a surviving Incan structure that was built in the 1400s.

In Peru, people sometimes decorate llamas as a sign of respect.

Over the centuries, llama populations have gradually increased. In the early 2000s, the llama industry began doing so well that some American farmers began choosing llamas over traditional farm animals such as sheep, chickens, or cows. For many people who live in the Andes, llamas and alpacas are still important livestock.

PURPOSE

Just like the ancient llamas, llamas today are strong pack animals. They can carry about 25 percent of their body weight. They adapt easily to different types of terrain.

Llamas often refuse to carry weights that are too heavy.

Llamas' hair can grow up to 10 inches (25.4 cm) long.

Llamas are intelligent and easy to train for many tasks. By repeating an action just a few times, they will quickly pick it up and remember it. This includes behaviors such as pulling a cart or carrying a pack. They can also be trained to do jobs like hauling firewood.

Llamas also serve as a source of wool. Llama fur is valued for its softness and warmth. The fibers can be used alone or blended with traditional wool from sheep. Llama wool can be used to make yarn, blankets, and other items. Colors range from black to white, with shades of beige, brown, and red. The wool may be solid or spotted.

Farmers sometimes use llamas as guardians for other livestock. When placed with sheep or goats, a llama will see itself as one of the herd. As the largest animal, it will act as the protector. Llamas will charge and stomp when dogs or coyotes approach. When an unknown human approaches, they may also let out a loud scream.

Farmers can keep llamas in large herds.

CARE

As social creatures, llamas do best when kept with other llamas. They will form strong bonds within their herd. Spitting is part of a llama's body language. Sometimes llamas use it to establish their social order within the herd.

Llamas need ample safe outdoor space to roam and graze. A well-fenced pasture helps make sure they get enough exercise. It keeps them safe from predators.

Like cows, llamas chew their cud. This means they swallow their food to be digested and bring it back up to chew some more before swallowing again.

Because llamas come from naturally cool climates, they are not used to areas with high heat and humidity. To avoid heat stress, they must have access to shade from trees or a shelter. Farmers can keep llamas cool by removing their wool or hosing them off. A llama's shelter should have a dirt floor or another slip-resistant material to prevent injuries to its sensitive feet. To keep llamas comfortable, farmers should provide dry, clean straw for bedding inside the shelter.

Llamas eat shrubs, trees, and flowering plants. But their main source of nutrients comes from foraging grasses, clover, and alfalfa. Farmers should pay attention to all plants in the pasture. Some plants are toxic to llamas and must be removed.

Foxglove is one plant that is toxic to llamas.

OSTRICHES

The common ostrich is the largest bird in the world. It can grow up to 9 feet (2.7 m) tall and weigh more than 330 pounds (150 kg).

Ostriches are large, flightless birds native to Africa. The domestication of ostriches began in South Africa during the 1800s. At this time, South Africa was under British rule.

Ostriches have large feathers called plumes. The plumes and smaller feathers were an important part of British fashion trends. They adorned the hats and clothing of fashionable women. Ostrich farms in South Africa became the main source of these feathers.

The first ostriches were imported from Africa to the United States in the late 1880s. This marked the beginning of ostrich farming in the United States. People wanted to make money from the growing demand for ostrich feathers.

However, during the early 1900s, fashion trends began to change. The demand for ostrich feathers declined. The ostrich farming industry did too. By the 1930s, many ostrich farms had shut down.

In the 1980s, ostrich leather was in demand. During this time, South Africa was controlled by a racist government. The United States limited trade with South Africa, and supply of ostrich products was suddenly cut off. As a result, ostriches in the United States became very valuable.

Ostrich feathers can be up to 30 inches (76 cm) long.

Wild ostriches live 30 to 40 years, while those in captivity live an average of 50 years.

People also discovered that ostriches produce red meat similar to beef but with less fat and cholesterol. As a result, ostrich farming experienced a comeback in the United States in the 1990s. Today Americans are still raising ostriches on farms. But South Africa remains the world leader, supplying 75 percent of all ostrich products worldwide.

PURPOSE

One of the main products ostriches are raised for is their meat. Ostrich meat is a healthier choice than other types of

red meat. It has also become a popular meat with chefs who want to offer unique and healthful foods.

Ostrich oil is another valuable product. It is rich in fatty acids and vitamins. Ostrich oil is used in the cosmetics and pharmaceutical industries. It is also used for skin care and hair care products because of its moisturizing properties.

Ostrich cream is sold to relieve muscle pain.

The skin of ostriches is used to create leather. Ostrich leather is known for its distinctive pattern and durability. It is an ideal material for making items such as boots, purses, and wallets. Items made from ostrich leather are expensive fashion products.

People still purchase ostrich feathers. But feathers aren't as commonly used in fashion. Today most ostrich feathers are used to clean fine machinery and equipment. They can reach

The bumps on ostrich leather are where the feathers grew.

and remove dust and debris from tight spaces without causing damage.

Ostrich eggs are about 20 times larger than chicken eggs.

Ostrich eggs are another product that comes from these large birds. The shells of ostrich eggs are often carved into intricate ornaments. Some eggs are used as beautiful containers, while others are made into decorative jewelry.

CARE

Ostriches on a farm need space to roam and exercise. Farmers should provide from 1 to 3 acres (0.4 to 1.2 ha) per bird. Ostriches need protection from the weather. They should have a three-sided shelter or barn that is large enough to keep them dry.

Ostriches can run up to 45 miles per hour (72 kmh).

In colder climates, the shelter should be heated in winter. Ostriches must stay inside if the ground is icy. They have only two toes, one large toe and one smaller stabilizing toe. They are more likely to slip on the ice than other birds.

Ostriches are strong and fast, so secure fencing is important. Farmers must use fencing that stands at least 6 feet (1.8 m) tall to keep ostriches in. The fencing must be sturdy. When ostriches are startled, they may run into the fence.

Ostriches feed mostly on grasses and crops such as corn. However, many farmers also supply their birds with commercial feed. The feed contains nutrients ostriches need. In the United States, alfalfa is the best source of nutrition available, so it makes up most of the feed. Since ostriches are desert animals, they need much less water than other livestock.

Captive ostriches eat about 3 pounds (1.4 kg) of food a day.

PIGS

Pigs originally descended from wild boars that roamed from Southeast Asia to western Europe. The wild boars were first domesticated in western Asia around 8500 BCE and in China around 6500 BCE. These domesticated pigs eventually made their way to Europe. Farmers allowed them to roam freely. They bred with European wild boars. By the 4000s BCE Europe had its own strain of domesticated pigs.

The Spanish explorer Hernando de Soto was the first to establish a herd of pigs in the Americas. In 1539 CE he brought 13 pigs with him to what is now Florida. The settlers and American Indians used them as a source of meat.

Yorkshire pigs are the most common breed on American farms.

A female pig gives birth to an average of 12 piglets in a litter.

Within three years, de Soto had more than 700 pigs. De Soto is known as the Father of the American Pork Industry.

Pigs reproduced quickly throughout the American colonies. By 1660 there were thousands of pigs in the colony of Pennsylvania alone. By about 1700, many farmers owned four or five pigs. Settlers moving westward took pigs with them. As the pig populations continued to grow, meat packing plants began springing up in large cities.

Pig barns can hold more than 1,000 hogs.

The states in the middle of the nation are known as the Corn Belt. This is because corn and other crops grow there. Farmers found that feeding their pigs these crops produced the most meat on the pigs for the least amount of money. They shipped the young pigs to these states for finishing. The Corn Belt became known as the Hog Belt. Today Iowa is still the largest state in pork production.

PURPOSE

Pigs provide valuable products for people all over the world. People use nearly every part of the pig. Little is wasted.

There are hundreds of different pig breeds. When choosing a breed, some people consider the personality. They want a pig that is easy to handle. Some pigs grow faster than others. Some pigs reproduce well. The taste of the meat also varies.

One of the main products is meat. The meat from pigs is called pork. Pork is high in protein and other important nutrients. Pork products include bacon, ham, sausage, pork chops, and other cuts.

People in the United States eat more than one billion pounds of bacon every year.

Pigs are raised until they reach slaughter weight. This is usually around 250 pounds (113 kg). On commercial farms, they reach this weight by the time they are six to eight months old.

Pigs provide many other types of products too. For example, their skin is used to make purses, shoes, luggage, and footballs. Their hair is used to make high-quality paintbrushes

Youth can raise pigs through a program called 4-H and show the pigs at fairs.

An enclosed barn is important to keep pigs warm in cold weather.

and brooms. Bones are made into buttons, glass, and glue. Pig fat is called lard. It is used in cooking, baking, and making soap.

Products from pigs are also a part of important medical and health products. These animals contribute ingredients for many drugs and pharmaceuticals. These include insulin, a substance used to manage diabetes. Pig heart valves are used to replace damaged human heart valves.

CARE

Pigs require a dry and comfortable shelter to protect them from bad weather. An insulated shelter with straw bedding helps keep them warm during cold seasons. Pigs benefit from separate areas within their enclosures for eliminating, exploring, and sleeping.

The average pig eats 5 to 7 pounds (2.3 to 3.2 kg) of food a day.

Pigs are known for their curiosity, and they are very strong. They must have a sturdy fence to prevent escape. The fence should be able to withstand their forceful pushing.

People commonly give pigs some slop. This is a mixture of food scraps and leftovers. But pigs should primarily eat a well-balanced diet. The bulk of a pig's diet should come from grains. Corn provides the pigs with energy, while soybeans provide protein. Other grains like wheat and sorghum can also be included. This type of diet will help the pigs grow and stay healthy.

Pigs do not have sweat glands. This means they can easily overheat, especially in warm weather. Farmers should provide a mud wallow or a shallow pool of water for their pigs. This allows them to cool down by wallowing, or rolling and relaxing, in it. This natural behavior helps regulate their body temperature.

Pigs usually begin wallowing at temperatures of 63 to 70 degrees Fahrenheit (17 to 21°C).

QUAIL

Male quail, *left*, have more markings than female quail, *right*.

Quail are the smallest farm birds. Some of them weigh as little as 3.5 ounces (100 g) when they are fully grown. In the wild and on the farm, quail live on the ground.

The Japanese quail is the species usually found on farms. These birds were first domesticated in Japan in the 1000s CE. The Japanese kept quail as songbirds.

Quail did not arrive in Europe until the 1950s. People began breeding them for their meat and their eggs. At first quail were raised to release on large estates. Wealthy people wanted to hunt them for sport.

Since then, quail have gained more popularity as a source of food worldwide. People in Asia and Mexico enjoy eating quail eggs. Quail meat is a standard dish in Europe. In the United States, people eat quail in fine restaurants.

Today there are about 70 domesticated quail breeds. The domesticated quail behave like wild quail. However, they have lost their instinct to migrate.

Quail are 3 to 20 times smaller than chickens.

PURPOSE

Quail meat is a healthier choice compared to other types of poultry. It is high in protein and low in fat. It also has important nutrients such as iron, zinc, and vitamin B12. There are many different varieties of domesticated Japanese quail. The Texas A&M is the most popular meat quail breed in the United States. It is fully grown in just seven weeks. Pharaoh D1 is the best egg producer. This quail can lay 300 eggs in one year.

Quail eggs are very small. It takes about three quail eggs to equal the size of one chicken egg. Quail eggs contain lower cholesterol and fat than chicken eggs. People who have egg allergies can often eat quail eggs.

The pattern on quail eggs helps hide them from predators.

Farm quail live an average of five to six years.

One of the biggest differences between quail and chicken farming is the time it takes for the birds to produce. Chickens usually start laying eggs around 18 to 26 weeks of age. However, quail are fully grown at just six weeks old. At eight weeks old, they are ready to be butchered. They are also already laying eggs. By the time a chicken starts to lay, a quail would have already laid as many as 120 eggs.

In the wild, quail live in groups of 8 to 25, so captive quail can be kept in groups.

CARE

Quail can be raised on small farms in a limited space. Some people raise them indoors in a basement, a spare room, a greenhouse, or a garage. A hutch or cage keeps them contained. Quail need about 1 square foot (0.1 sq m) of space per bird. Their hutch should provide a place to lie down, since quail do not perch.

Quail can be kept outdoors too. Because they can fly, farmers must plan their enclosures with this in mind. High fences or covered tops can prevent the quail from escaping.

If they get out of the pen, they are in danger of being caught by many different predators.

Quail should have nesting boxes in which to lay their eggs. The boxes should be cozy, quiet spaces. These boxes will help keep the eggs safe and will also make it easier for the farmer to collect them.

Most of the world's farm quail are raised in China.

RABBITS

Domesticated rabbits come from the European rabbit. The earliest written records of captive rabbits go back to ancient Rome. The Romans built hutches for the animals. Remains of rabbits have been discovered from the first century CE.

In about 600 CE, French monks tamed wild rabbits. They were to be used as a substitute for other meat during religious fasting periods. By the Middle Ages, only the nobility ate rabbits. As people began transporting rabbits across Europe, they became a popular delicacy. They were also highly valued for their fur.

Rabbits can see almost 360° around them.

During the 1500s, people began documenting changes in rabbit fur color. This marked the beginning of selective breeding. People wanted rabbits with certain desirable traits. This eventually led to the development of different rabbit breeds.

Domesticated rabbits were imported to the United States by the 1840s. They were a popular source of meat until the 1960s, when people began eating more beef. Today chefs and their customers are again becoming interested in locally raised rabbit meat. There are currently 49 recognized breeds.

The Flemish Giant rabbit is the largest rabbit breed in the world.

Rabbits native to the Americas have never been domesticated. This is because American rabbits are not social animals. They live alone and often fight with each other.

PURPOSE

The main product rabbits provide is meat. Rabbits are usually slaughtered when they reach approximately 5 pounds (2.3 kg) and are about ten weeks old. This ensures that the meat is tender and flavorful. Buyers of rabbit meat include restaurants,

In 2021, the world produced 949,905 tons (861,739 metric tons) of rabbit meat.

Angora wool is used to make sweaters, gloves, scarves, and other items.

custom meat stores, and individuals. Rabbit meat is high in protein and low in fat, cholesterol, and sodium, making it a healthful choice. Popular meat breeds include the California rabbit, New Zealand rabbit, and American chinchilla rabbit.

Angora rabbits are fiber-producing animals. Their wool is combed, plucked, or clipped when ready to shed. The wool is then spun into high-quality, expensive yarn to make clothing and other items. English, French, and Satin Angoras can yield 10 to 16 ounces (280 to 450 g) of wool per year. Giant Angora rabbits can produce 28 to 40 ounces (790 to 1,130 g) of wool in a year.

The practice of raising rabbits for meat and wool is called *cuniculture*.

Rabbits also contribute to the farm by providing fertilizer. Farmers can raise earthworms and keep them in rabbit manure piles. The worms turn the manure into nutrient-rich compost. This makes excellent natural fertilizer for plants.

CARE

There are many ways to house rabbits on a farm. They can live in indoor or outdoor hutches. The housing should keep the rabbits safe from bad weather and predators.

Rabbit hutches should be made mostly of wire. Rabbits chew on wooden cages. Hutches should also be kept clean and get plenty of light. Grown male and female rabbits should have their own individual cages. This is so they do not breed when the farmer does not want them to. Young rabbits may be kept together in one pen.

Baby rabbits are usually weaned from their mother's milk between 30 and 45 days after birth.

When a female rabbit is ready to give birth, a nest box should be placed in the hutch. The box provides privacy for the doe, or female, and protection for the kits, or baby rabbits. The box can be made of wood, wire, or metal. Straw or wood shavings make good bedding for the box.

If an area is secure and safe from predators, rabbits

If rabbits don't get enough exercise, they won't grow properly.

A rabbit owner with a yard can sometimes find safe wild plants such as clover to feed his or her rabbit.

can spend time outside. This gives them a chance to exercise and eat from more natural food sources, such as grasses and some clover. Rabbits raised this way produce more meat of higher quality than rabbits that stay in hutches.

Rabbits also need hay and grain or commercial pellets. The pellets have all of the nutrients rabbits need. Farmers should avoid feeding Angora rabbits hay. The dust from the hay can get into the rabbit's wool and lower its quality. All rabbits enjoy greens as a treat.

REINDEER

Reindeer and caribou are the same species, *Rangifer tarandus*. Wild and domesticated reindeer live in Europe and Asia. Wild caribou are found in North America. Wild reindeer originally lived in the tundra and forests of northern Russia and Scandinavia. The oldest document describing domesticated reindeer came from the 800s CE. In a letter, Norse explorer Ohthere of Hålogaland mentions a herd of more than 600 reindeer.

The average male reindeer weighs between 140 and 550 pounds (64 and 250 kg), depending on the season.

Farmers can use dogs to herd reindeer.

In the 1700s, diseases in Iceland killed more than half of the country's sheep. Because people used the sheep for meat, much of the food supply was gone. To help, reindeer were brought over from Norway. But most people weren't interested in raising reindeer. However, the reindeer thrived in the wild.

Domesticated reindeer were first introduced in the United States during the late 1800s. Whaling ships off the coast of Alaska had killed many marine mammals. These animals were an important food source for the Indigenous people of Alaska. To help them, reindeer were shipped in from Siberia in 1891. Soon after, Scandinavians came to Alaska to teach reindeer herding.

The average adult reindeer eats 9 to 18 pounds (4.1 to 8.2 kg) of food a day.

The reindeer population in Alaska grew. By the 1920s, there were approximately 400,000 reindeer. Processing and shipping reindeer meat became one of the most important industries in Alaska. By the 1930s, the reindeer population reached around 640,000. Seeing the success of the reindeer in Alaska, the Canadian government decided to set up reindeer farms. In 1929 herders led a group of reindeer from Alaska to the Northwest Territories in Canada. They would help feed starving people in the western Arctic.

Today there are only about 20,000 reindeer on farms in Alaska. But farmers are also raising reindeer in most parts of the United States. These farms go as far south as Texas, Mississippi, and Tennessee. Russia, Finland, Norway, and Canada also have domesticated reindeer farms.

Wild caribou are generally slightly larger than domesticated reindeer.

PURPOSE

People still raise reindeer for their meat. Reindeer meat is high in protein and vitamins. It is low in fat. The meat is often compared to fish in terms of nutrition.

Milk is another food product that comes from reindeer. It has a much higher fat content than cow milk. The fat content of reindeer milk is 24 percent. The fat content of cow milk is only 4 percent. Reindeer milk is also higher in protein. This helps calves grow quickly, since summer in the Arctic is short. Fermented reindeer milk is used to make many types of cheese.

The soft covering on new reindeer antlers is called velvet.

Reindeer-pulled sleighs used to be a main transportation option for people in northern Scandinavia. Today some people enjoy using this mode of transportation to race.

Reindeer hides and antlers are used for decorations. Reindeer calves begin growing antlers within weeks of birth. Both males and females grow antlers. Most drop their antlers in the winter. Pregnant females retain their antlers until spring. This helps them protect food sources for themselves and their growing calves through the winter.

Farm-raised reindeer are friendly and easy to train. They may be part of Christmas parades or displays. Reindeer can pull a sleigh for special events.

Adult reindeer can swim up to 6 miles per hour (9.7 kmh).

CARE

Reindeer are easy to handle. They can be kept in small spaces compared to other animals of their size. In the summer, reindeer need shaded shelters and large bodies of water to keep cool. Reindeer can swim across rivers or lakes. Their large, broad hooves work well as paddles.

Reindeer are cold-weather animals and stay outside through the winter. Fur covering a reindeer's body helps it stay warm in its very cold habitat. Reindeer even have fur on the bottoms of their hooves. This helps them keep from slipping on icy ground.

A reindeer's diet includes grasses, shrubs, and more than 200 other kinds of plants. In winter, reindeer eat mainly lichens, organisms made up of fungi and algae that grow on rocks, logs, and trees. Lichens can make up 40 to 90 percent of a reindeer's diet. Reindeer can also eat grass and alfalfa hay. Some farmers give their animals commercial feed to make sure they're getting the right nutrients.

Owners must be watchful for changes in their reindeer's behavior. These animals don't show symptoms of sickness until they are very ill. By then, it may be too late to save them.

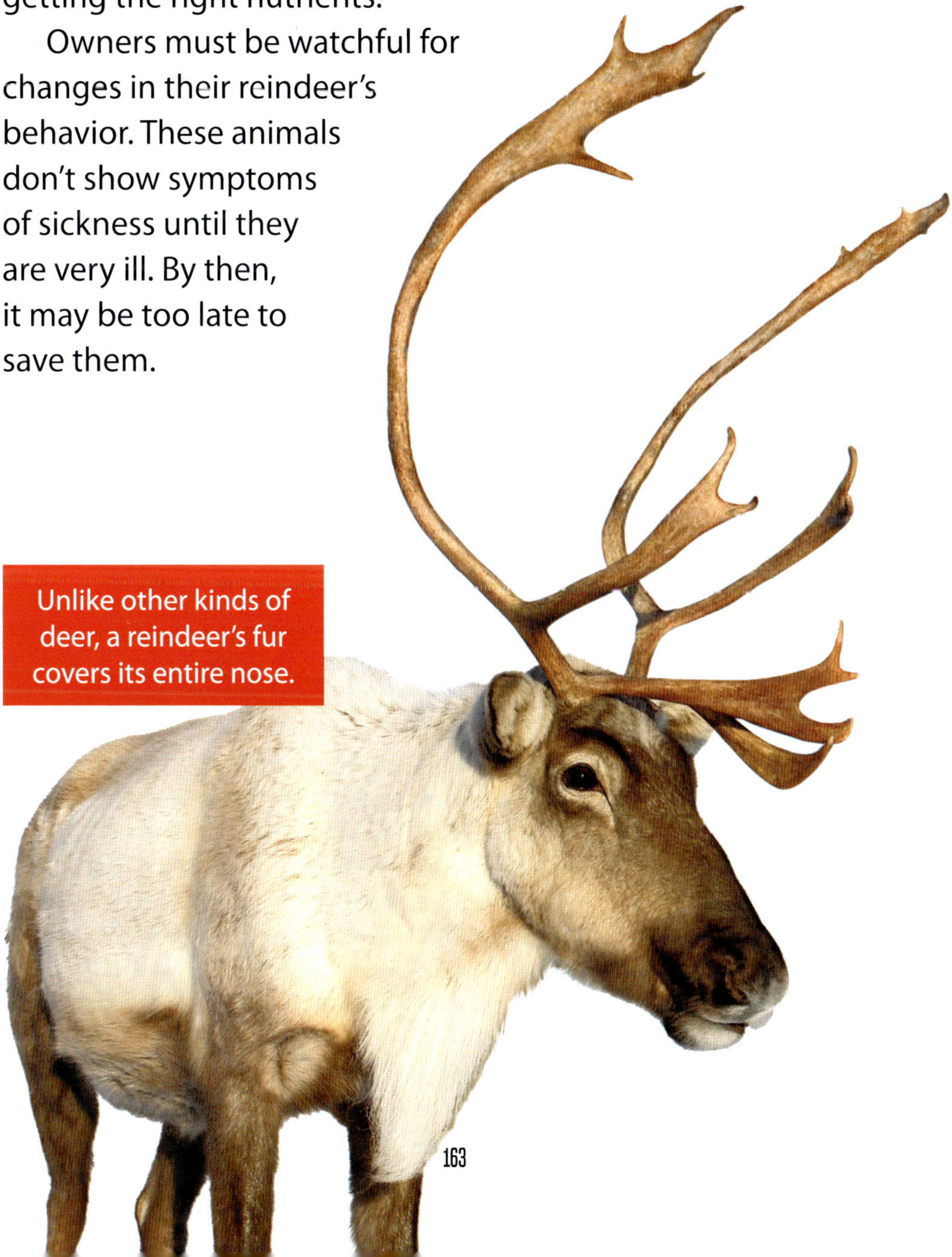

Unlike other kinds of deer, a reindeer's fur covers its entire nose.

SHEEP

Male sheep, *right*, are called rams and female sheep, *left*, are called ewes.

Sheep have been raised by people for thousands of years. The sheep on farms today originated from wild sheep. During the Bronze Age, people in Mesopotamia began breeding sheep to have denser fleeces. They also wanted white fibers. Over time, sheep with these types of coats spread throughout western Asia.

Sheep were a part of the ancient Greek and Roman cultures. Writings by the ancient Greeks describe breeding sheep and creating wool fabric. They mention sheep farms with as many as 10,000 sheep. Sheep from Asia were also introduced to North Africa and Europe.

During the Middle Ages, the wool trade flourished in Europe. The merino breed was introduced in Spain in the 1100s. It was so valuable to the Spanish that selling one merino sheep to another country was punishable by death. But as the Spanish Empire declined during the 1700s, the sheep were given away or sold. Merino sheep continued to spread through Europe, Asia, and Australia during the 1700s and 1800s.

Merino sheep can produce fleeces weighing up to 40 pounds (18 kg).

In 2023 there were 5.2 million sheep and lambs on US farms.

Christopher Columbus brought Spanish sheep to the Americas in the 1490s. These sheep became the ancestors of today's Navajo-churro breed. Spanish explorers brought sheep through Mexico and the western United States. Today most US sheep farms are located in the West. China has more sheep than any other country.

PURPOSE

The two main products that come from sheep are meat and wool. The majority of sheep raised in the United States are raised for meat. Most of the sheep raised in Australia are raised for wool. Australia sells more wool than any other country.

Shearing a sheep can take as little as two minutes.

Sheep are able to recognize human faces.

There are more than 1,000 breeds of sheep. Some breeds are better suited for their meat. Meat sheep are categorized by their age. The term *lamb* refers to any sheep that is less than 14 months old. Yearlings are usually between one and two years old. Sheep are over two years old.

Most lambs are slaughtered when they are almost one year old. Cuts of lamb meat include lamb chops, rack roast, sirloin, and leg of lamb. If the sheep is more than one year old, the meat is called mutton.

In the United States, Suffolk is the breed most commonly raised for meat. It is known for its high quality. Other popular meat sheep breeds include Dorper and Hampshire. These breeds are easy to care for. This makes them a good choice for smaller farms. Hair sheep grow short hair instead of wool. They are also used for meat.

Sheep produce different types of wool depending on the breed. Fine-wool sheep have wool made up of very soft, thin fibers. Rambouillets are fine-wool sheep. Coarse-wool sheep have thick fibers. Romneys and Lincolns are coarse-wool breeds. Medium-wool sheep have wool that falls between the fine and long wool. A Dorset sheep is a medium-wool sheep.

Rambouillet

Dorset

Romney

CARE

Sheep prefer a diet of grass and clover. They do well with just grazing in a pasture. Usually they do not need any extra grain. Sheep that don't have a lot of pasture can also be given hay.

Sheep need shelter to get out of harsh weather conditions. A shelter can be a three-sided structure. A barn-type structure that can be closed at night helps protect the sheep from predators. Major predators are coyotes and dogs. However, it is better to have an open, cold, dry barn rather than one that is warm and damp. Sheep can become sick in a damp barn.

Sheep have four-chambered stomachs. This helps them digest grass.

Overgrown sheep hooves can make walking painful.

Sheep need special care from time to time. Their hooves must be trimmed at least twice a year. Sheep's hooves are constantly growing. In the wild, a sheep would naturally wear them down. But in pastures, they do not get worn down enough. Trimming the hooves keeps them even and comfortable.

Most sheep grow wool continuously. Every spring, their coats must be sheared. This way they stay cool during the summer.

TURKEYS

Wild turkeys are native to the eastern and southwestern United States, as well as to parts of Mexico. Indigenous people in Mexico and Central America were probably the first to domesticate turkeys. Archaeologists have uncovered evidence of domesticated turkeys in Mexico as early as 800 BCE.

A turkey's head can change color based on its mood.

The broad-breasted white turkey is the most common turkey raised in the United States.

Spanish explorers arrived in Mexico in the 1500s CE. At the time, native people known as the Aztecs lived in northern Mexico. In 1511 explorers took domesticated turkeys back to Europe and introduced them in Spain. At first, turkeys were expensive birds that only very wealthy people kept and bred. European royalty and aristocracy began raising turkeys on their large estates. Over time they became a more common farm bird.

In the early 1600s, English colonists brought domesticated turkeys back to the Americas. These birds crossbred with the native wild turkeys. The offspring were the color of the wild turkeys, and many were larger than the European ones. By the late 1800s, farmers had developed many different turkey breeds.

Turkey eggs, *bottom*, need incubators to operate at around 100 degrees Fahrenheit (38°C).

By the late 1910s, the methods of raising turkeys began to change. Most farmers now hatched the eggs in artificial incubators. But after hatching, turkeys still roamed freely and were considered partially wild. Around this time, an American farmer named Charles Wampler had an idea. He built an incubator and hatched the first chicks in 1922. He raised them completely in captivity. Wampler became known as the Father of the Modern Turkey Industry. Today the United States produces about 280 million turkeys every year.

PURPOSE

Turkeys are raised for their meat. Turkey meat provides protein, vitamins, and minerals. It is also low in fat. The United States is the world's largest turkey producer. Americans prefer the white meat of turkeys. But most people in other countries prefer dark meat.

There are different varieties of domesticated turkeys. The broad-breasted white turkey is the main turkey in large-scale production in the United States today. This variety came from many years of selective breeding. Broad-breasted whites have white feathers and more meat than many other turkey breeds. They are ready to go to market when they are 16 weeks old.

In the United States, turkey is commonly enjoyed during the Thanksgiving holiday.

Heritage turkeys are any of several breeds of domesticated turkeys. They have characteristics of wild turkeys that are no longer seen in the broad-breasted whites. These include a variety of feather colors, smaller size, and slower growth rate. Broad-breasted whites grow to about 20 pounds (9.1 kg) in 16 weeks. Heritage turkeys grow to 18 pounds (8.2 kg) in 28 weeks.

The Narragansett turkey is a kind of heritage turkey.

Heritage turkeys need at least 3 square feet (0.3 sq m) of space per bird.

Turkeys also produce eggs for farmers. They are slightly bigger than chicken eggs. The shells are also tougher. Turkeys do not lay eggs as often as chickens. They also must be raised longer before they begin to lay. This means that it costs more to produce turkey eggs. For this reason, turkey eggs are not a popular food item.

CARE

Like other types of farm birds, turkeys need a secure coop at night. This helps protect them from predators. In the coop, broad-breasted turkeys need a roost that is low to the ground. Otherwise they may injure their legs or feet when jumping down from the roost.

Heritage turkeys have an instinct to sleep up high. They like to have a good view of their surroundings. These turkeys do better in a barn instead of a coop. The shelter can take a variety of forms. But it should have a roof and at least two sides that protect from the rain, snow, and wind.

Turkey enclosures can have a lot of dust, so it is important for farmers to wear masks to protect their lungs while inside.

After 14 weeks, the average turkey eats around 1 pound (0.45 kg) of feed a day.

Some American farmers raise turkeys in scientifically designed barns. The turkeys do not go outside. Instead, the barns are ventilated and kept at comfortable temperatures. Living in the barns provides protection from outside threats, such as predators, disease, and extreme weather.

In the wild, a turkey's diet consists of fruits, insects, and seeds. Heritage turkeys are set loose to eat grass and insects and are fed some grains. Broad-breasted turkeys eat a diet of corn and soybean meal mixed with extra vitamins and minerals. This way of feeding turkeys produces the large birds people buy in grocery stores.

WATER BUFFALO

Water buffalo resemble cattle.

Water buffalo can be found in both Africa and Asia. African water buffalo, also known as Cape buffalo, are not domesticated. Asian water buffalo were domesticated thousands of years ago. Today there are fewer than 4,000 Asian water buffalo left in the wild.

There are two types of Asian water buffalo. These are the river buffalo and the swamp buffalo. The swamp buffalo was domesticated in southern China, Indochina, and Southeast Asia between 5000 and 1000 BCE. The river buffalo was native to India. It was domesticated in approximately 4000 BCE. Over thousands of years, people migrated and took the buffalo with them. By the early Middle Ages, the river buffalo had spread as far as Egypt, Greece, and Italy. The swamp buffalo eventually reached Malaysia, Indonesia, central China, Taiwan, the Philippines, and Borneo. Today water buffalo can be found in approximately 50 countries.

Special hooves keep water buffalo from sinking underwater in mud.

Water buffalo first reached North America in 1975. That year, researchers at the University of Florida thought water buffalo might help with a weed problem. Aquatic weeds filled the waterways in the southeast United States. The water buffalo ate the weeds. A magazine article about the success in Florida

Water buffalo need space to graze.

Water buffalo are used to plow rice fields.

caught the attention of a man named A. P. Leonards. He imported 53 swamp buffalo and 96 river buffalo. Since then, the water buffalo population in the United States has increased to a few thousand.

PURPOSE

Water buffalo are often referred to as the Living Tractor of the East. This is because many people in Asia rely on them for plowing and transportation. The water buffalo's pulling power makes up 20 to 30 percent of the total farm power in Southeast Asia. Swamp buffalo are used mostly for pulling.

A water buffalo produces about 0.5 gallons (1.9 L) of milk a day.

River buffalo are raised mainly for milk. Water buffalo produce between 5 and 15 percent of the world's milk. The largest buffalo milk producers are India, Pakistan, and China. Buffalo milk contains 40 percent more protein, 58 percent more calcium, and 43 percent less cholesterol than cow milk.

Buffalo milk has a high amount of milk solids. This means that less buffalo milk is needed to make the same amount of cheese as cow milk. A cheese called buffalo mozzarella is made from buffalo milk. It is the water buffalo's best-known product. Other dairy products include yogurt, ricotta cheese, feta cheese, kefir, butter, and gelato.

Some people raise water buffalo for their meat. Water buffalo meat is leaner than beef. It contains half of the cholesterol and one-fourth the amount of fat. The hides of buffalo can be made into high-quality leather.

CARE

Water buffalo vary in size based on their environment. Where food is scarce, the buffalo tend to be smaller. Water buffalo need enough space to roam and graze. But water buffalo are highly adaptable to their environment. Their digestive systems are more efficient than those of cows. This means that they can do well on average-quality forage. In colder climates in the winter, buffalo also need special feed.

Water buffalo leather is used to make wallets, bags, and boots.

Housing for buffalo should protect the animals from harsh weather. They need a place to escape the rain, snow, and strong winds. In cooler parts of the country, buffalo need insulated barns. In the summer, the animals need shade. Buffalo also like to wallow in mud. The mud helps keep them cool.

Water buffalo are much stronger than cows. That means their fences must be much sturdier than typical fences. Water buffalo can be easily raised in many parts of the world. They are resistant to many common diseases. This helps keep vet bills lower.

Water buffalo need extra protection when temperatures drop below 40 degrees Fahrenheit (4.4°C).

Water buffalo are social animals.

GLOSSARY

compost
A nutrient-rich mixture of decayed organic matter such as food scraps, grass, and leaves.

cosmetics
Products people put on their skin, hair, nails, or teeth to make them feel more beautiful.

delicacy
Food that is delightful or rare.

digestive enzyme
A protein that helps a chemical reaction take place. This reaction breaks down food into nutrients during digestion.

domesticated
Relating to a living thing that has changed over time to suit the needs of humans or benefits from living with humans.

durable
Strong and lasts a long time without breaking or becoming weaker.

feral
Relating to a domesticated animal that has escaped captivity and adapted to live in the wild again, or relating to this animal's offspring.

forage
Food that animals eat while grazing or browsing; to search for food.

hatchery
A place for breeding and raising fish in a controlled and captive setting.

herbicide
A substance used to kill unwanted plants such as weeds.

humidity
Water vapor or moisture in the air.

incubate
To keep eggs warm until it is time to hatch.

Indigenous
Relating to the people who originally lived in a particular country or region.

lactose
A sugar found in milk.

pasteurization
The heating of a substance for a certain length of time in order to kill most of the harmful bacteria.

pharmaceutical
Relating to medicines.

toxic
Poisonous.

TO LEARN MORE

FURTHER READINGS

Castaldo, Nancy. *Ultimate Food Atlas*. National Geographic Kids, 2020.

Dinmont, Kerry. *The 4-H and FFA Encyclopedia*. Abdo, 2025.

Garcia, Merriam. *The Dog Encyclopedia*. Abdo, 2021.

ONLINE RESOURCES

Booklinks
NONFICTION NETWORK
FREE! ONLINE NONFICTION RESOURCES

To learn more about farm animals, please visit **abdobooklinks.com** or scan this QR code. These links are routinely monitored and updated to provide the most current information available.

INDEX

Africa, 30, 33, 38, 70, 72, 78, 102, 126, 164, 180
  South Africa, 104, 126–128
American Indians, 22, 24, 134
Andes, 6–7, 118–121
Asia, 30, 38, 46, 54, 63, 71–72, 78, 94, 110, 134, 142, 156, 164–165, 180, 183
  China, 38, 57, 78–80, 86, 95, 134, 167, 180–181, 184
  India, 180, 184
Australia, 31, 103, 165–167

bedding, 37, 85, 125, 139, 154
breeding, 6, 22, 47–50, 64–65, 72, 88, 90, 94, 102, 110, 134, 142, 148, 164, 173, 175
breeds, 8, 42, 46–48, 50, 55–56, 58, 65–67, 79, 81–82, 94, 96, 104–106, 111, 113, 137, 143–144, 148–149, 151, 165–169, 173, 175–176

cleaning, 27, 130, 153
commercial farming, 4, 49, 56, 58, 61, 79–80, 88–89, 101, 138
coops, 59–60, 177–178

dairy, 47–49, 52–53, 104–105, 184
  cheese, 48, 105, 160, 184
  milk, 30, 34, 47–49, 52, 105, 160, 184
domestication, 6, 22, 27, 30–31, 38, 46, 54, 62, 70–72, 78, 94–95, 102, 110, 118, 126, 134, 142–144, 148–150, 156–157, 159, 172–173, 175–176, 180

eggs, 54–58, 60, 82, 88, 94, 97, 131, 142–145, 147, 174, 177
Egypt, 14, 39, 54, 78, 94–95, 181
Europe, 14, 22, 38, 40, 46–48, 54, 63, 72, 78, 86–88, 94, 104, 110, 119, 134, 142–143, 148, 156, 164–165, 173
  France, 148, 151
  Spain, 46, 102, 119, 134, 165–167, 173

feathers, 81, 94, 96, 98, 101, 126–127, 130, 175–176
fencing, 12, 27, 29, 36–37, 50, 68, 108–109, 124, 132, 140, 146, 186
Fertile Crescent, 38, 102
fiber, 5, 35, 106, 122, 151, 164, 169
fleece, 6–11, 13, 164
flocks, 56, 59, 94, 99–100

grass, 12, 25, 50–52, 76, 99, 113, 125, 132, 155, 162–163, 170, 179
Great Plains, 23

hay, 12, 25, 52, 76, 108, 116, 155, 163, 170
herds, 11, 13, 23–24, 27–29, 46, 50, 63, 65–66, 102, 109, 118, 123–124, 134, 156–158
hides, 22, 27, 30, 118, 161, 184
hives, 14, 17–18, 20–21
honey, 14, 16–18, 20–21

Inca, 7, 119

meat, 5, 10–11, 23–26, 30, 34, 47–50, 53, 56–58, 79–81, 94, 96, 98, 104, 106, 118–119, 128–129, 134–137, 142–144, 148–151, 155, 157–158, 160, 167–168, 175, 184
Mediterranean, 14, 39, 63

North America, 15, 22, 78, 94, 104, 156, 182

pack use, 31–33, 70, 72, 74, 118, 121–122
predators, 12, 29, 37, 59, 63, 65, 67, 69, 73, 85, 108, 124, 147, 152, 154, 170, 177, 179

shearing, 13, 171
shelters, 12, 22, 29, 37, 38, 43, 45, 50, 76, 85, 108, 115, 125, 131–132, 139, 162, 170, 178
  barns, 12, 43–45, 53, 76, 108, 131, 170, 178–179, 186
  sheds, 43, 108, 115
slaughter, 11, 25, 49–52, 57, 96, 98, 138, 150, 168
South America, 6, 78, 111, 118

wool, 6, 9, 11, 31, 118, 122, 125, 151, 155, 164–169, 171

PHOTO CREDITS

Cover Photos: Sviatlana Laza/Shutterstock Images, front (chicken); Shutterstock Images, front (horse, goat, pig, ostrich, duck), back (llama); Daniel Prudek/Shutterstock Images, front (bees); Eric Isselee/Shutterstock Images, front (cow, alpacas); Yanlei Zhang/Shutterstock Images, front (sheep); Aksenova Natalya/Shutterstock Images, back (turkey)
Interior Photos: Eric Isselee/Shutterstock Images, 1, 6, 22, 30 (bottom), 43, 49, 77, 94, 102, 104, 118, 151, 164 (left); Mariliis Kutsar/Shutterstock Images, 2–3, 48–49; Hananeko Studio/Shutterstock Images, 4; Shutterstock Images, 5, 12, 14, 17, 21, 31, 34, 40, 41, 42, 45, 50 (right), 57, 60, 62–63, 64, 65, 70, 79, 81, 85, 92, 93, 95, 105, 106, 111, 115, 117, 122, 125, 134–135, 135, 138, 140–141, 142, 149, 150, 153, 156, 159, 160, 162, 164 (right), 166, 167, 169 (middle), 170, 176, 177, 181; Franck Camhi/OSTILL/Shutterstock Images, 7; Mercedes Lamborelle/Shutterstock Images, 8–9; Rita Kochmarjova/Shutterstock Images, 9, 109, 154–155; Boumen Japet/Shutterstock Images, 10; Luis Salazar Bonilla/Shutterstock Images, 11; Joann Randles/Cover Images/AP Images, 13; Iryna Rasko/Shutterstock Images, 15; Jennifer Bosvert/Shutterstock Images, 16; Mirko Graul/Shutterstock Images, 18; Serenko Natalia/Shutterstock Images, 19; Olga Kok/Shutterstock Images, 20; DEA Picture Library/De Agostini/Getty Images, 23; Paul Maguire/Shutterstock Images, 24–25; Brent Hofacker/Shutterstock Images, 25; Waltraud Grubitzsch/dpa-Zentralbild/ZB/picture alliance/Getty Images, 26; Kenneth D. Love/Shutterstock Images, 27; Patrick Pleul/dpa-Zentralbild/ZB/picture alliance/Getty Images, 28–29; David Osborn/Shutterstock Images, 29; Artorn Thongtukit/Shutterstock Images, 30 (top); William Hunton/Shutterstock Images, 32; Grace Wangui/Shutterstock Images, 32–33; Irina Mavritsina/Alamy, 35; Vinnikava Viktoryia/Shutterstock Images, 36; Elena Odareeva/Shutterstock Images, 37; Arco Bianco/iStockphoto, 38; Ashmolean Museum/Heritage Images/Hulton Archive/Getty Images, 39; Walt Bilous/Shutterstock Images, 44; Florilegius/Universal Images Group/Getty Images, 46; Rachel Hoover/Shutterstock Images, 47; Mara Ze/Shutterstock Images, 50 (left), 56; Jeffrey Schwartz/Shutterstock Images, 51; Joe Sohm/Visions of America/Universal Images Group/Getty Images, 52–53; Philipp Schulze/dpa/picture alliance/Getty Images, 53; Ram Jagan/Shutterstock Images, 54–55; Werner Forman/Universal Images Group/Getty Images, 55; Nataliia Iliuk/Shutterstock Images, 58 (left); Ton Bangkeaw/Shutterstock Images, 58 (right); Davor Ristic/Shutterstock Images, 59; Alexander Lipko/Shutterstock Images, 60–61; Natallia Yaumenenka/Shutterstock Images, 62; Dora Zett/Shutterstock Images, 66; Farlap/Alamy, 67; Maria Moroz/Shutterstock Images, 68; Ariel Celeste Photography/Shutterstock Images, 68–69; Sokolova Alla/Shutterstock Images, 71; Delmas Lehman/Shutterstock Images, 72–73; Lee Kay/Shutterstock Images, 73; Angela Meier/Shutterstock Images, 74; Drago Nika/Shutterstock Images, 75; Dietrich Leppert/Shutterstock Images, 76; Maria Grin/Shutterstock Images, 78; Don Emmert/AFP/Getty Images, 80–81; Natthawut Ngoensanthia/Shutterstock Images, 82; Kuttelvaserova Stuchelova/Shutterstock Images, 83; Aleksandr Kondratov/Shutterstock Images, 84; Iaroshenko Maryna/Shutterstock Images, 86; Universal History Archive/Universal Images Group/Getty Images, 86–87; Jim Lane/Education Images/Universal Images Group/Getty Images, 88–89; Yichuan Cao/NurPhoto/Getty Images, 89; Tatjana Baibakova/Shutterstock Images, 90; Vladislav Gajic/Shutterstock Images, 91; Konstantin Ampleev/Shutterstock Images, 96; Tatevosian Yana/Shutterstock Images, 97; Dan Olsen/Shutterstock Images, 98; Chokniti Studio/Shutterstock Images, 98–99; Alvarez/E+/Getty Images, 100; Alamin Khan/Shutterstock Images, 100–101; Dave Primov/Shutterstock Images, 103; Yurii Maslak/Shutterstock Images, 106–107; Orphi Eulenforst/Shutterstock Images, 108–109; Lyubov Levitskaya/Shutterstock Images, 110; Alexia Khruscheva/Shutterstock Images, 112; Dale A. Stork/Shutterstock Images, 113; Martin Charles Hatch/Shutterstock Images, 114; LightField Studios/Shutterstock Images, 116; Anton Ivanov/Shutterstock Images, 119; Thomas Wyness/Shutterstock Images, 120; Irina Mos/Shutterstock Images, 121; Jess Kraft/Shutterstock Images, 123; Lisa Stelzel/Shutterstock Images, 124; Sanit Fuangnakhon/Shutterstock Images, 126–127; Yana Vasileva/Shutterstock Images, 127; Uwe Anspach/dpa/picture alliance/Getty Images, 128–129; Kingma Photos/Shutterstock Images, 129; AJStudio Photography/Shutterstock Images, 130; Sergey Ryzhov/Shutterstock Images, 131; Natascha Kaukorat/Shutterstock Images, 132; Joe Zybernatic/Shutterstock Images, 133; Mai Chayakorn/Shutterstock Images, 136–137; Sergiy Kuzmin/Shutterstock Images, 137; Tim Belyk/Shutterstock Images, 139; Tengku Naufal/Shutterstock Images, 141; Iaroslav Konnikov/Shutterstock Images, 143; Alexey Kabanov/Shutterstock Images, 144; Africa Studio/Shutterstock Images, 145; Wirakorn Deelert/Shutterstock Images, 146; Zhang Ailin/Xinhua News Agency/Getty Images, 147; Jiang Hongyan/Shutterstock Images, 148; Sergey Lavrentev/Shutterstock Images, 152; Kolomiyets Viktoriya/Shutterstock Images, 155; Sergey Anisimov/Anadolu Agency/Getty Images, 156–157; Nik Norzawani Nik Zakaria/Shutterstock Images, 158; Vladimir Kovalchuk/Shutterstock Images, 161; Sylvie Bouchard/Shutterstock Images, 163; John Carnemolla/Shutterstock Images, 164–165; Chubykin Arkady/Shutterstock Images, 168; Larry Mayer/The Billings Gazette/AP Images, 169 (top); Susan Pilcher/Shutterstock Images, 169 (bottom); SCP Photography/Shutterstock Images, 171; Aksenova Natalya/Shutterstock Images, 172; Jennifer Yakey-Ault/Shutterstock Images, 173; Maryna Pugachova/Shutterstock Images, 174; Bochkarev Photography/Shutterstock Images, 175; John Tlumacki/Boston Globe/Getty Images, 178–179; Violeta Marculescu/Shutterstock Images, 179; Thanakorn Hongphan/Shutterstock Images, 180; Derek Davis/Portland Press Herald/Getty Images, 182–183, 187; LilyRose Photos/Shutterstock Images, 183; Wut Moppie/Shutterstock Images, 184; Gil Cohen Magen/Shutterstock Images, 185; Alexandr Junek Imaging/Shutterstock Images, 186

ABDOBOOKS.COM
Published by Abdo Reference, a division of ABDO, PO Box 398166, Minneapolis, Minnesota 55439.

Printed in China.
052024
092024

THIS BOOK CONTAINS RECYCLED MATERIALS

Editor: Marie Pearson
Series Designer: Colleen McLaren
Production Designers: Joshua Olson, Laura Kuchar

LIBRARY OF CONGRESS CONTROL NUMBER: 2023949525

PUBLISHER'S CATALOGING-IN-PUBLICATION DATA
Names: Bell, Samantha S., author.
Title: The farm animal encyclopedia / by Samantha S. Bell
Description: Minneapolis, Minnesota: Abdo Reference, 2025 | Series: Farming encyclopedias | Includes online resources and index.
Identifiers: ISBN 9781098294328 (lib. bdg.) | ISBN 9798384913597 (ebook)
Subjects: LCSH: Livestock--Juvenile literature. | Animal husbandry--Juvenile literature. | Farm animals--Juvenile literature. | Domesticated animals--Juvenile literature. | Agriculture--Juvenile literature. | Farming--Juvenile literature. | Encyclopedias and dictionaries--Juvenile literature.
Classification: DDC 636--dc23